Ghost Stories 1

Dennis Pepper

OXFORD
UNIVERSITY PRESS

OXFORD
UNIVERSITY PRESS

Great Clarendon Street, Oxford OX2 6DP

Oxford University Press is a department of the University of Oxford.
It furthers the University's objective of excellence in research, scholarship,
and education by publishing worldwide in

Oxford New York

Athens Auckland Bangkok Bogotá Buenos Aires Calcutta
Cape Town Chennai Dar es Salaam Delhi Florence Hong Kong Istanbul
Karachi Kuala Lumpur Madrid Melbourne Mexico City Mumbai
Nairobi Paris São Paulo Singapore Taipei Tokyo Toronto Warsaw
and associated companies in Berlin Ibadan

Oxford is a registered trade mark of Oxford University Press

This selection and arrangement copyright © Dennis Pepper 1994

The moral rights of the author have been asserted

These stories first published in *The Young Oxford Book of Ghost Stories* 1994
First published in paperback 1996
Reprinted 1997, 1998, 1999
First published in this paperback edition 2000

British Library Cataloguing in Publication Data available

ISBN 0 19 275020 8

2 4 6 8 10 9 7 5 3

Typeset by AFS Image Setters Ltd, Glasgow

Printed in Great Britain
by Cox & Wyman Ltd, Reading, Berkshire

Contents

The Rivals

VIVIEN ALCOCK

John Pearce was a clever boy. Every Speech Day would find him, blinking modestly behind his thick spectacles, trotting up to the platform to receive prize after prize into his thin, eager hands. Everyone said he would go far—though probably not on his feet, which were flat as Dover soles, and inclined to smell fishy in hot weather. His English teacher, sounding the only sharp note in a chorus of praise, said he had no imagination, but this was not quite fair. John believed in many things he had not seen: atoms and molecules, microbes and magnetic fields. He did not, however, believe in ghosts.

So when the milkman told them, the morning after he and his parents had moved into their new home, that the house next door was haunted, he laughed and said,

'What rot! I don't believe in ghosts.'

'John is so sensible,' his mother said. She stepped outside and peered at the houses on either side. 'Which one?' she asked, with an enjoyable shiver.

It was, of course, the one on the left, the sinister side:

1

a dark house, the colour of dried cat's meat, its sly, gothic windows masked with heavy Nottingham lace. No clear light of day or reason could penetrate those dingy cotton flowers and flourishes into the hidden rooms behind. Put in some picture windows, and white nylon net, John thought, and there'd be no more talk of hauntings.

The house had changed hands six times in the last three years, the milkman told them, handing over two bottles, white as ghosts. No one could stand it any longer. All that screaming and wailing, footsteps and icy draughts of air. Cost a fortune just trying to keep it warm! The present owners had been there only five weeks. 'Got it dirt cheap,' he said. 'Thought they were getting a bargain, poor devils. I give them six months.'

After breakfast, Mrs Pearce shooed John out into the garden, saying she could manage better on her own. No, he was not to go up to his room and stick his nose into a book. He worked too hard at his studies. The sunlight and fresh air would do him good. He was looking pale.

John wandered down the neat concrete path, examined the aphids on the roses with a critical eye, murmured the Latin names of all the plants he recognized, and made a note to look up those he did not. Then, with nothing left to do, he climbed onto a tree stump and looked over the high wall into the garden next door.

On a neglected lawn, ankle-deep in daisies and dandelions, a young girl was standing, bouncing a ball against the thick trunk of a chestnut tree. A pretty girl, with a face like a flower and long dark curling hair.

His heart sank a little: he could have wished she were plain. It was not that he disliked pretty girls, far from it, but he knew from experience that they did not like him. His learning did not impress them. His clever remarks, his carefully prepared jokes, fell flat. They giggled behind their hands, called him Four Eyes, and yawned in his face when he tried to share his knowledge. All the time he was speaking to them, he could see their eyes skittering across the classroom to some good-looking thick-head on the other side. Pretty girls, he thought glumly, were always stupid.

Yet he was so lonely. He would have liked a friend. Perhaps she had brothers? He thought hopefully of a quiet, studious boy, like himself. They could go round the Science Museum together, not just rushing around pressing buttons to make things light up, but slowly and seriously. They could collect pondlife in jam jars, and study it under his microscope. They could have picnics in his room, discussing the theories of Pythagoras by candlelight. If only she had such a brother . . .

'Hallo,' he called.

The girl started and dropped her ball, which vanished in the long grass. Then she smiled and came towards him. 'Hallo,' she said.

'I'm John Pearce. We've just moved in.'

'Yes. I know.'

'What's your name?'

'Lucy Wilkins.'

There was a little silence. She seemed shy. He studied her. Her eyes were remarkable: a pale, sparkling blue, cool as water, and fringed with long black lashes. Her voice was clear and sweet, and rather posh. Perhaps she went to a boarding school and was lonely in the holidays. Perhaps she too would be glad of a friend. It was a pity she was pretty, and, QED, bound to be stupid.

He asked her if she had any brothers or sisters, and was disappointed when she shook her head.

'I'm an only child too,' he said. And for a moment, because she was so pretty, he hoped (foolishly, he knew) that she would say, 'Let's be friends. I've always wanted a brother. It's lonely on your own.' But she did not, of course. She simply smiled and said nothing. Already she was looking bored, and her eyes were sliding away from him, glancing back at the dark house as if even its gloomy privacy would be better than his company. Any moment she would make an excuse—she had to help with the dishes or the dusting, or wash her hair. He wished he could think of something to say to keep her there . . .

'Have you seen any good ghosts recently?' he asked humorously.

'Oh, you've heard already!' she said crossly. 'Who told you that—'

'That your house was supposed to be haunted? The milkman. Icy draughts, strange wailings, footsteps in the night; all the usual old rubbish . . . You don't mean you believe in it, do you?' he asked.

She stared back at the dark house and shivered. 'Yes.'

Poor silly girl, he thought. He explained to her kindly that there were no such things as ghosts. Icy draughts in an old house were only to be expected. 'You should buy some plastic filler and seal up the cracks.'

She looked sulky and mumbled, 'You don't know what it's like.'

As for the footsteps . . . He went on to explain about the expansion and contraction of old floorboards, affected by temperature and humidity.

She sniffed, and stuck out her lower lip.

And the wailing, he said, that would be wind in the chimneys.

It was funny. You would think people would be glad

to have their fears and worries explained away in a rational manner, but they never were. He was not surprised when, instead of looking grateful, she merely scowled.

'It is haunted! It is! I know it is!' she said stubbornly.

He laughed. 'Have you ever seen a ghost? Actually *seen* one?'

'*Yes!*'

The little liar! 'What did it look like?'

She hesitated.

Caught her there. She's got no more imagination than I have, John thought with satisfaction.

'Oh, horrible, horrible,' she muttered at last, obviously unable to think of anything better. 'Wicked! And it's me it's after. I know it is! It wants to drive me out . . . Oh, it's easy for you to laugh! You're safe next door.'

'I suppose it walks when the moon is full?'

She nodded. 'In that room,' she said, pointing to a top window overlooking the garden. 'At midnight, that's when it comes. Searching, looking for *me*!'

'Why don't you just lock the door and shut it in?'

'There's no key,' she said, and her voice trembled, 'for a door like that.'

Poor silly, pretty little fool! She really was frightened, he thought, and his heart filled with a warm, protective love that he had only felt once before, when he had seen a little white mouse in his father's laboratory. Wanting to comfort her, he offered to stay all night in the haunted room.

'I'm not afraid,' he said, and she looked at him with huge eyes, as if unable to believe anyone could be so brave. Or so foolish.

'The moon is full tonight,' she whispered.

They decided not to tell their parents. Parents, John informed her, could never be relied on not to produce objections to the most innocent and harmless schemes.

At ten to midnight, John knocked softly on the side door of the haunted house. It opened immediately. She must have been waiting behind it. Her face was as pale as a lily in the shadows.

'Come,' she whispered, and led the way upstairs. Softly though he trod, the stairboards creaked and groaned beneath his feet. If anyone hears, John thought, they'll take us for ghosts. But he didn't want to be caught. It might be difficult to explain . . .

'Have your parents gone to bed yet?' he whispered.

'Yes. A long time ago.'

They went up two flights of stairs, along a narrow passage, and then Lucy opened a door. It creaked. The hinges need oiling, he thought.

Now they were in a large room. Bright moonlight struggled through the thick lace curtains, patterning the floor with wriggling little worms of light. John tiptoed across to the window and pushed them back.

'That's better,' he said, and looked round. There was no furniture, and the floor was carpeted only with dust. The wallpaper was dark. Opposite the window, a large mottled mirror, in a heavy frame, gleamed dully in the moonlight. On the left, there was a pale marble fireplace, an empty grate, and two cupboards in the alcoves on either side. He opened each door in turn and shone his torch inside. Empty. Dirty. Dusty.

'No wonder your ghost only visits once a month,' he whispered, grinning, 'if this is the room you give it.'

Lucy did not answer. She was sitting in a corner, with her arms wrapped around her. He could see the whites of her eyes as she kept glancing nervously from the door to the window and back again.

In the garden, an owl hooted. It was very cold. Strangely cold for a summer night.

'That's because it's a corner house,' John explained. 'It catches the wind both ways. Draughty.' And he told her about air currents and wind velocity. He did not know if she was listening. Her eyes still moved from the door to the window, and back again.

A clock began to strike twelve. The curtains flared wildly at the window. The house creaked and shuddered. There was a thin wailing from the garden below.

'The wind's coming up,' John said. 'They said on the radio the weather was going to change.'

Now there were screams, wild, despairing, unearthly.

'Cats,' John said, and began to tell Lucy about the mating habits and aggressive displays of cats . . .

'Look!' she whispered.

The door was opening, slowly, slowly. A figure appeared. Thin as a candle, it flickered into the moonlight. Its face was grey and gaunt, its white gown all spattered and splashed with blood.

'How d'you do,' John said, getting to his feet and blinking at it short-sightedly. 'Are you Lucy's mother?'

It drifted towards him, moaning and wringing its hands. Its eyes were burning like coals in its ashen face.

'Aren't you feeling well?' John asked, uneasily. He took off his glasses and wiped them on his handkerchief. But when he put them on again, there was no improvement. The lady (for it appeared to be a female) looked dreadful. 'Can we get you anything? An aspirin?' He looked towards Lucy for help, but she was cowering in her dark corner, and did not move.

7

'Oh, I am murdered, murdered!' the lady wailed. 'Murdered in my bed!'

A joke! A practical joke! They had planned it together to make a fool of him.

'Ha! Ha! Very funny,' he said, furious that they should have thought him so gullible. 'But I'm sorry. It's wasted on me. I don't believe in ghosts. And I'm afraid it's time I was getting back. I promised to help Mum in the morning.'

'Murdered!' the lady repeated, staring at him with hollow eyes. 'Murdered in my bed, the wicked devils!'

He stared back at her stolidly, refusing to be frightened, and a look of impatience came into her ravaged face. 'Murdered,' she repeated slowly, as if to a backward child. 'October the second, it was, in the year of disgrace, 1872.'

'That's a long time ago. I should forget it if I were you,' John said stoutly, and was surprised how high his voice sounded, almost like a scream. It seemed a long way to take a practical joke. It occurred to him that perhaps the lady was mad.

'Don't you believe me?' the apparition asked, her icy breath chilling his cheek.

'No,' he said. His pulse was racing now. He was burning and shivering. It wasn't fear, he told himself. He must be sickening for something.

'Look at me!' She came nearer, and John backed away until he was against the wall.

He did not want to look at her. His glasses must be misting up in the freezing air, and that was why her face seemed to be melting, dripping from her bones like candle wax.

'Oh, please! You must believe in me, you must!' the

lady moaned. 'Even the gods die for want of faith. I need your fear. I can only exist in your mind. Oh, please believe in me, or I am lost.'

'I'm sorry,' John said stubbornly, his teeth chattering. 'I don't believe in ghosts. I don't! I won't!'

The figure seemed to dwindle, fading away like smoke.

'Please,' it wailed faintly. 'Oh, please believe in me.'

John was shaking all over now, but he managed to say, 'No.'

'Oh, I am murdered, murdered, murdered,' sighed the ghost, its voice failing. Then it was gone.

The boy, his back to the wall, slid slowly down till he was sitting on the floor. His face was white, fixed, terrified.

'She's gone! She's gone! You did it!' the girl cried, smiling and clapping her hands together.

'It—it was a trick!' he babbled. 'I know it was! You had a hidden projector! A video tape! It's just a trick! You had something up your sleeve!'

The girl was dancing on the floor. Her feet made no sound on the bare boards. They left no prints in the dust. Now she danced in front of the mirror, and there was no reflection. Her eyes were shining, literally shining, like twin lamps. As John watched her in terror, she cried gloatingly, 'It's mine! All mine now! The whole house! She's gone, that horrible creature. Always scolding. Always criticizing. Saying I shouldn't walk in the sun. Saying I didn't know how to haunt properly, just because she's been dead longer than I have. Why should I care for her silly rules? I'll show her! Oh, I'll be *ghastly*!'

She came dancing towards him, and she was all moonlight.

'Thank you, thank you, thank you,' she whispered. 'I love you.'

And she vanished.

As he sat staring at the empty room, he felt an icy touch on his lips, as soft and wet as a snowflake.

He never saw her again. The two houses were sold within the year, and a block of flats built where they had stood. John and his parents moved to the other side of town. He grew up, won more prizes, and became rich and famous, and happy enough. But he never married. Sometimes, on a summer night, he would stand by his window, and sniff the sweet smell of night-scented stocks, and see the pale roses glimmering in the moonlight. Then he would smile and say,

'A pretty girl once loved me.'

The Monkeys

RUSKIN BOND

I couldn't be sure, next morning, if I had been dreaming or if I had really heard dogs barking in the night and had seen them scampering about on the hillside below the cottage. There had been a Golden Cocker, a Retriever, a Peke, a Dachshund, a black Labrador, and one or two nondescripts. They had woken me with their barking shortly after midnight, and made so much noise that I got out of bed and looked out of the open window. I saw them quite plainly in the moonlight, five or six dogs rushing excitedly through the bracken and long monsoon grass.

It was only because there had been so many breeds among the dogs that I felt a little confused. I had been in the cottage only a week, and I was already on nodding or speaking terms with most of my neighbours.

Colonel Fanshawe, retired from the Indian Army, was my immediate neighbour. He did keep a Cocker, but it was black. The elderly Anglo-Indian spinsters who lived beyond the deodars kept only cats. (Though why cats should be the prerogative of spinsters, I have never been able to understand.) The milkman kept a couple of mongrels. And the Punjabi industrialist who had bought a former prince's palace—without ever occupying it—left the property in charge of a watchman who kept a huge Tibetan mastiff.

None of these dogs looked like the ones I had seen in the night.

'Does anyone here keep a Retriever?' I asked Colonel Fanshawe, when I met him taking his evening walk.

'No one that I know of,' he said, and he gave me a swift, penetrating look from under his bushy eyebrows. 'Why, have you seen one around?'

'No, I just wondered. There are a lot of dogs in the area, aren't there?'

'Oh, yes. Nearly everyone keeps a dog here. Of course every now and then a panther carries one off. Lost a lovely little terrier myself, only last winter.'

Colonel Fanshawe, tall and red-faced, seemed to be waiting for me to tell him something more—or was he just taking time to recover his breath after a stiff uphill climb?

That night I heard the dogs again. I went to the window and looked out. The moon was at the full, silvering the leaves of the oak trees.

The dogs were looking up into the trees, and barking. But I could see nothing in the trees, not even an owl.

I gave a shout, and the dogs disappeared into the forest.

Colonel Fanshawe looked at me expectantly when I met him the following day. He knew something about those dogs, of that I was certain; but he was waiting to hear what I had to say. I decided to oblige him.

'I saw at least six dogs in the middle of the night,' I said. 'A Cocker, a Retriever, a Peke, a Dachshund, and two mongrels. Now, Colonel, I'm sure you must know whose they are.'

The Colonel was delighted. I could tell by the way his eyes glinted that he was going to enjoy himself at my expense.

'You've been seeing Miss Fairchild's dogs,' he said with smug satisfaction.

'Oh, and where does she live?'

'She doesn't, my boy. Died fifteen years ago.'

'Then what are her dogs doing here?'

'Looking for monkeys,' said the Colonel. And he stood back to watch my reactions.

'I'm afraid I don't understand,' I said.

'Let me put it this way,' said the Colonel. 'Do you believe in ghosts?'

'I've never seen any,' I said.

'But you have, my boy, you have. Miss Fairchild's dogs died years ago—a Cocker, a Retriever, a Dachshund, a Peke, and two mongrels. They were buried on a little knoll under the oaks. Nothing odd about their deaths, mind you. They were all quite old, and didn't survive their mistress very long. Neighbours looked after them until they died.'

'And Miss Fairchild lived in the cottage where I stay? Was she young?'

'She was in her mid-forties, an athletic sort of woman, fond of the outdoors. Didn't care much for men. I thought you knew about her.'

'No, I haven't been here very long, you know. But what was it you said about monkeys? Why were the dogs looking for monkeys?'

'Ah, that's the interesting part of the story. Have you seen the *langur* monkeys that sometimes come to eat oak leaves?'

'No.'

'You will, sooner or later. There has always been a band of them roaming these forests. They're quite harmless really, except that they'll ruin a garden if given half a chance . . . Well, Miss Fairchild fairly loathed those monkeys. She was very keen on her dahlias—grew some prize specimens—but the monkeys would come at night, dig up the plants, and eat the dahlia bulbs. Apparently they found the bulbs much to their liking. Miss Fairchild would be furious. People who are passionately fond of gardening often go off balance when their best plants are ruined—that's only human, I suppose. Miss Fairchild set her dogs at the monkeys, whenever she could, even if it was in the middle of the night. But the monkeys simply took to the trees and left the dogs barking.

'Then one day—or rather, one night—Miss Fairchild took desperate measures. She borrowed a shotgun, and sat up near a window. And when the monkeys arrived, she shot one of them dead.'

The Colonel paused and looked out over the oak trees which were shimmering in the warm afternoon sun.

'She shouldn't have done that,' he said. 'Never shoot a monkey. It's not only that they're sacred to Hindus—but they are rather human, you know. Well, I must be getting on. Good-day!' And the Colonel, having ended his story rather abruptly, set off at a brisk pace through the deodars.

I didn't hear the dogs that night. But next day I saw the monkeys—the real ones, not ghosts. There were about twenty of them, young and old, sitting in the trees

14

munching oak leaves. They didn't pay much attention to me, and I watched them for some time.

They were handsome creatures, their fur a silver-grey, their tails long and sinuous. They leapt gracefully from tree to tree, and were very polite and dignified in their behaviour towards each other—unlike the bold, rather crude red monkeys of the plains. Some of the younger ones scampered about on the hillside, playing and wrestling with each other like schoolboys.

There were no dogs to molest them—and no dahlias to tempt them into the garden.

But that night, I heard the dogs again. They were barking more furiously than ever.

'Well, I'm not getting up for them this time,' I mumbled, and pulled the blankets over my ears.

But the barking grew louder, and was joined by other sounds, a squealing and a scuffling.

Then suddenly the piercing shriek of a woman rang through the forest. It was an unearthly sound, and it made my hair stand up.

I leapt out of bed and dashed to the window.

A woman was lying on the ground, and three or four huge monkeys were on top of her, biting her arms and pulling at her throat. The dogs were yelping and trying to drag the monkeys off, but they were being harried from behind by others. The woman gave another bloodcurdling shriek, and I dashed back into the room, grabbed hold of a small axe, and ran into the garden.

But everyone—dogs, monkeys and shrieking woman—had disappeared, and I stood alone on the hillside in my pyjamas, clutching an axe and feeling very foolish.

The Colonel greeted me effusively the following day.

'Still seeing those dogs?' he asked in a bantering tone.

'I've seen the monkeys too,' I said.

'Oh, yes, they've come around again. But they're real enough, and quite harmless.'

'I know—but I saw them last night with the dogs.'

'Oh, did you really? That's strange, very strange.'

The Colonel tried to avoid my eye, but I hadn't quite finished with him.

'Colonel,' I said. 'You never did get around to telling me how Miss Fairchild died.'

'Oh, didn't I? Must have slipped my memory. I'm getting old, don't remember people as well as I used to. But of course I remember about Miss Fairchild, poor lady. The monkeys killed her. Didn't you know? They simply tore her to pieces . . . '

His voice trailed off, and he looked thoughtfully at a caterpillar that was making its way up his walking stick.

'She shouldn't have shot one of them,' he said. 'Never shoot a monkey—they're rather human, you know . . . '

Mayday!

REDVERS BRANDLING

Captain Ian Sercombe was frightened. He rested a broad forefinger on the control column of the Boeing 747 and eased back in his seat. Glancing out of the cabin windows at the sixty metres of his giant machine's wingspan he tried to calm himself with thoughts of its size and detail . . . as high as a six storey building, over two hundred kilometres of wiring, four million parts, space for more than four hundred passengers . . .

'Decent night, Skip.'

First Officer Les Bright's voice cut in on Ian's thoughts. The two men had completed the pre take-off check and were sitting on the flight deck. Outside a huge moon hung in the hot tropical night sky which pressed down on Singapore's Changi Airport.

Les Bright was talking to the control tower when Cabin Service Director Edwina Reeves came into the flight deck area.

'Two hundred and sixty passengers and thirteen cabin crew all safely on board, Captain. Cabin secure.'

'Thanks, Edwina,' replied Ian. 'We should be off very soon.'

Minutes later the huge aircraft began to roll away from its stand at the airport. The time was 8.04pm and the journey to Perth, Australia had begun.

Within an hour all was routine on the flight deck. The Jumbo was cruising at Flight Level 370, about seven miles above sea level. Speed was 510 knots and the course was 160° magnetic as the plane, under the automatic pilot, headed south over Indonesia.

'Weather ahead looks good,' commented First Officer Bright, nodding at the weather radar screen which promised three hundred miles of smooth flying ahead.

'Hmmm,' agreed Ian.

He had been studying the weather radar with unusual intensity—just as he had all the other complex instruments in the cabin. But the fear wouldn't go away. It wasn't nervousness . . . or apprehension . . . Ian Sercombe was frightened. He could only ever remember feeling like this once before, and that had been the dreadful day of the accident . . .

Ian and his lifelong friend Mike Payne had been crewing together on a flight back from New York. Leaving the airport in Ian's car, they were accelerating on the M25 when a tyre burst. In the crash which followed Ian had been unhurt, but Mike was killed instantly. Just before the tyre went Ian had felt this unreasoning fear. Afterwards he could never quite rid himself of guilt for Mike's death. He'd been blameless perhaps—he'd checked the tyres just a couple of days previously—but how could Mike know that? Once again he thought of Mike's bluff, smiling Irish face, grinning as always and clapping those gloved hands together. Always been a joke between them that—the only pilot who never flew without wearing fine kid gloves.

Ian's thoughts were brought back to the present as First Officer Bright made a routine position report.

'Jakarta Control, Moonlight Seven over Halim at 20.44.'

Then it started.

'Unusual activity on weather radar, Captain.'

'I see it, Les.'

'Just come up—doesn't look good.'

'Could be some turbulence in that. Switch on the ''Fasten Seat Belts'' sign.'

The two pilots tightened their own seat belts. Behind them in the crowded cabins, passengers grumbled as they had to interrupt their evening meal to fasten their seat belts. Smiling stewardesses assured them there was no problem.

'Engine failure—Four!'

The flight engineer's terse voice cut the flight deck silence.

'Fire action Four,' responded Ian simultaneously.

Together Les Bright and Engineer Officer Mary Chalmers shut off the fuel lever to Four and pulled the fire handle. There was no fire in the engine and Ian felt an easing of his tension.

No pilot likes an engine failure, but the giant Jumbo could manage well enough on the three that were left.

'Engine failure Two.'

Mary Chalmers' voice was more urgent this time, but as she and Les Bright moved to another emergency procedure she suddenly gasped breathlessly.

'One's gone . . . and Three!'

Seven miles high with two hundred and seventy-three people on board, the Boeing was now without power. Ian knew that the huge plane could only glide—and downwards.

'Mayday, Mayday, Mayday!' First Officer Bright's voice barked into the emergency radio frequency. 'Moonlight Seven calling. Complete failure on all engines. Now descending through Flight Level 360.'

Ian's hands and mind were now working with automatic speed. He again checked the fuel and electrical systems. Emergency restarting procedures failed to have any effect. Quickly he calculated their terrible position. The plane was dropping at about two hundred feet per minute . . . which meant that in twenty-three minutes' time . . .

'You two,' said Ian quietly to the First Officer and Flight Engineer. 'I'm going to need all the help I can get later on, but there could be problems back there with the passengers now—especially as we're obviously going down. Go back—help out—and get back here as soon as you can.'

Bright and Mary Chalmers climbed out of their seats, slamming the door to the flight deck behind them as they went to try and reassure the terrified passengers.

Ian was now alone on the flight deck.

'Problems,' he muttered aloud. 'Crash landing in the sea so keep the wheels up, lights are going to fail because there's no generated power from the engines, standby power from the batteries won't last long . . .'

The closing of the flight deck door interrupted Ian's monologue.

'All right back there?' he asked, as the First Officer climbed back into his seat. He was just able to make out his fellow pilot's quick nod in the rapidly dimming light on the flight deck.

'It's too risky to try and get over those mountains now,' said Ian. 'What do you think?'

'Go for the sea,' was the reply, in a strangely muffled tone.

Ian's arms were aching from holding the lurching and buffeting aircraft, but he was surprised when the First Officer leaned over and laid a hand on his shoulder. It seemed to have both a calming and strengthening effect.

'I'll take her for a while.'

The giant plane continued to drop. At 14,000 feet the emergency oxygen masks had dropped from the roof for passengers' use. Now the rapidly dropping height was down to 13,000 feet.

'I'll save myself for the landing,' muttered Ian, watching his co-pilot in admiration. In the dim light the First Officer was a relaxed figure, almost caressing the jerking control column. His touch seemed to have calmed the aircraft too. Its descent seemed smoother, almost gentle even.

13,000.

12,000.

11,000.

'Ian.'

The captain was startled by the unexpected use of his Christian name by the First Officer.

'Volcanic dust and jet engines don't mix. I think we should make another re-light attempt on the engines now.'

Still feeling calm, even relaxed considering the terrible situation they were in, Ian began the engine restarting drill yet again.

'Switch on igniters . . . open fuel valves . . . '

As suddenly as it had failed, Engine Four sprang back into life.

'We've got a chance!' cried Ian.

'Go for the rest,' was the quiet reply.

Expertly, Ian's hands repeated the procedure. There was a lengthy pause then . . . Bingo! Number Three fired. . . then One . . . and then Two.

'We'll make it after all,' sighed Ian, once again taking a firm grip of the controls.

'Les—get on to Jakarta Control and tell them what's happening . . . Les . . . '

To his astonishment, when Ian looked to his right only the gently swaying control column came into view. The First Officer had gone. It was then that the captain heard the crash of the axe breaking through the door to the flight deck.

Engineer Chalmers was the first one through the shattered door.

'Fantastic, Skipper, fantastic—how did you do it?'

'Incredible!'

This was Les Bright's voice.

'The flight deck door jammed and we've been stuck out there for five minutes wondering how on earth you were getting on—and now this! You're a marvel, Skipper.'

Ian glanced up at the animated face of his First Officer in the brightening light of the flight deck.

'But . . . '

The rest of the words died on his lips. A feeling of inexplicable gratitude and calm swept over him. He remembered the confident, sure figure who had so recently sat in the co-pilot's seat. He now remembered too that just before the lights had reached their dimmest he had noticed that the hands holding the controls were wearing a pair of fine kid gloves.

'Get on to Jakarta,' Ian said quietly. 'Tell them we're coming in.'

Fat Andy

STEPHEN DUNSTONE

Andrew and his mother were walking through St Leonard's churchyard, on their way back from the shops. It was a short cut they had been taking for the last forty years or so, and it was pleasanter than going by the road: there was the well-kept grass, the beautifully trimmed hedge, the daffodils in spring, the swallows nesting over the south transept window . . .

'That window's going to be filthy before long,' said Millie.

But Andrew's mind was not on swallows—he was grappling with a difficult thought. For the church was to be made redundant, and the important issue for Andrew— the thing Andrew was trying to puzzle out—was this: when would God's spirit actually leave? Would it be when the Bible and prayer books were removed, or would He wait until the roof fell in? Andrew had special reasons for wanting to know.

'I saw a damp patch in the vestry this morning,' Millie was saying. 'It's a leak in the plumbing, I expect. Wasn't

24

the roof, we haven't had rain. Might be the mains, under the floor.'

'Mains is off,' said Andrew.

'Doesn't mean you can't get water,' said Millie. 'You don't get water when the mains is *on* sometimes, so you could easily get it when it's off. You should look.'

'God's going,' said Andrew. 'Bad'll come.'

'Don't talk daft. God doesn't want dafties.'

He didn't answer.

'Oh, now would you look at that!' exclaimed Millie, as they passed a well-tended grave. 'Is that the cats been playing around? They've scattered all the flowers you put out. Would you believe it?'

But Andrew was panting away down the path, the shopping bag swinging against his legs.

He shut the church door behind him—rather loudly in his haste—and stood on the worn stone step, getting his breath back. He looked around the old walls, seeking reassurance. Yes: God was still here.

Safe now, he could let the pictures come into his head. They'd been coming a lot recently.

In the pictures a wave crashes on a rocky beach; two children are playing among the pools: a girl and a boy. No one else is in sight. The boy does not seem to be enjoying himself.

Their voices—her voice—is carried on the breeze: 'Can't catch me! Can't catch me!' Then, with a sudden burst of inspired rhyming: ' 'Cos you're much too FAT, got a face like a big cow PAT!'

But he has almost caught her. He lunges—a fat boy's lunge—she squeals and runs off across the rocks. 'FatAndyfatAndyfatAndyfatAndy . . . can't catch me . . . '

It seems he doesn't want to play any more; he turns to go back the way they came.

25

Instantly: 'Where are you going?' calls the girl. 'Come back! Spoil sport!'

But he plods resolutely along the shingle. The girl runs to catch him up.

'I didn't mean it,' she says. 'Please play.'

He ignores her.

'Honestly, you're really nice, I really think so.'

He falters.

She dangles bait. 'I want to show you something.' He stops, looks at her. 'It's a secret, it's a really special secret. Do you want to know?'

His look tells her he does, very much.

'Then you've got to catch me. I won't run too fast.' And she's off again; off down the beach and onto a rock, where— coquettishly, like some shore-bird in a mating display—she calls: 'Andy . . . Andy . . . Andy . . . Andy . . . '

He makes up his mind—he cannot live without the secret— and he trots after her. Instantly, she's away into the distance, calling into the wind: 'FatAndyfatAndyfatAndyfatAndy . . . '

The pictures faded, and Andrew blinked in the sunlight that shafted through the south transept window, undimmed by swallows' droppings.

He whispered to God: 'It wasn't cats. I've kept her sleeping, till now, but she knows, see. She knows you're going.'

The next day, Andrew was in the church again, with his mother, collecting hassocks and piling them up. Millie was looking out for the ones she had embroidered; Andrew was wondering if a bargain could be struck with God. If they left a hassock, and Andrew came and knelt on it, and if they left a prayer book and a hymn book somewhere, couldn't He be persuaded to stay? It wouldn't be like before, but He could pretend. Couldn't He?

'Aren't you going to go and look at that damp?' said Millie. 'It might be doing something in the crypt.'

'Not my job any more,' said Andrew petulantly.

'Someone'll have to look: you don't want a flood.' They carried on piling. 'I hope it's fine for the vicar's little speech tomorrow,' said Millie, after a while.

'Is it after that, God goes?' said Andrew. 'Is it what the vicar says?'

'It's nothing to do with the vicar, it's the bishop signing a paper, I expect.'

'I hope he never signs it,' said Andrew.

'You're soft in the head,' said his mother.

Outside, somewhere, a dog barked. Andrew dropped the hassock he was holding and looked up, ready for flight. 'What was that?'

'A dog, silly.'

'Wild dog?'

'Quite soft in the head,' said Millie. But he didn't hear her.

The girl and boy are walking side by side, close to the water, talking.

'Why are you fat?' asks the girl.

'Don't know,' says the boy, simply.

'I expect they could operate,' says the girl. 'My father says they can do anything in hospital. I expect they could slice bits off.'

'Don't want to go to hospital.'

'They'll have machines they can bring and do it at home for you.'

'Don't want machines.'

27

'I'd hate to be fat,' she says. 'I'm glad I'm beautiful. I won our class beauty competition. It's my bone structure.'

'Where are we going?' asks the boy. 'What's the secret you're going to show me?'

'Do you want to hold my hand?'

He thinks about it. 'All right.'

'Well you can't!' And she runs off again. ''Cos you're too fat! FatAndyfatAndyfatAndyfatAndy . . . '

At the appointed time, a handful of ancient faithfuls gathered in the churchyard to hear the vicar's little speech and see Andrew get his present. All those years of keeping the churchyard looking so nice: it was only proper he should get his thanks. The sun shone benignly down.

'His whole life,' the vicar was saying, 'has been dedicated to the service of simple beauty: witness his devotion to the remembrance of young Joanne, who was taken so untimely from her family all those many, many years ago. It is Andrew in his unquestioning faith and selflessness who has acted as a model to us all, tending the memory of a blessed innocent with the flowers of God's garden. I would love to say ''Long may it all continue thus'', but alas . . . '

And on he went, talking about dwindling congregations, straitened times, and the recent problem of subsidence. But Andrew wasn't listening. He was staring with widening eyes at a certain headstone. It was at a tilt, surely it was at a tilt. It hadn't been yesterday. His breath began to come fast and shallow. He turned, blundered past his mother, past the vicar and ancient faithfuls.

'Andrew!' bellowed his mother. 'Come back here, this is for you!' But he was gone, into his refuge.

Once inside, he leant his head against the wall, waiting

for his pounding heart to ease. He laid his cheek against the cool plaster, touched its solidity with his hands. He stood there without moving.

The girl must have waited for him to catch up, because they're walking together again.

'It must be very boring being called Andrew,' she says.

But he doesn't reply. So much of what she says confuses him. They walk on. Looking straight ahead of her, the girl says, 'I think you're in love with me.' His heart beats faster, but again he says nothing, and she rounds on him, almost ferociously: 'Are you?'

'Where are we?' says the boy. 'I don't know where we are.'

'You're stupid. I don't think I'm going to show you my secret any more,' she says, carelessly.

'Please.'

'I'm going to push you in the sea and watch you float away to America.'

He looks anxiously at her. 'Don't push me in.'

'I will. After three. One—'

'Don't!' He starts to run off. 'I'm going back, I don't want to see your secret, you're horrid.'

'No, I'm not, please, Andrew,' she calls. 'I won't be horrid again, cross my heart and hope to die, I promise I won't push you in.'

'I'll push you in.' But he has stopped running.

They stand on the rocks, facing each other.

'Shall we play kiss chase?' says Joanne.

Andrew sat at the foot of the stairs, staring unseeing at a spot on the hall carpet. The vicar'd said the church would have to be padlocked from tomorrow, and Andrew'd got upset, so his mother had had words with him: told him to pull himself together. But he *was* together, he didn't need pulling, she didn't understand; she didn't *know*. He didn't like it when his mother scolded him.

He sat up, aware suddenly that he could see her reflection in the hall mirror, standing on the stairs above him. He'd thought she was outside.

'Mother?' he said, to the reflection.

A voice that was not her voice spoke softly from behind him: 'Andrew . . . '

He leapt up in panic, turned to face the voice, but there was no one there. He rushed along the hall, through the kitchen and out of the back door.

'Mother, Mother, Mother,' he cried, in the garden.

'Yes, dear, I'm here, what's happened?'

'She . . . she . . . she . . . she . . . she . . . she . . . '

'Shh, there . . . '

'She . . . she . . . '

Millie put her arm around his quivering shape. 'Who, dear?'

'She was in there, she was you.'

'Who was, dear?'

'Joanne, she was pretending to be you. Is *this* you? You're not her still?'

'No, dear, I'm always me and no one else, especially when I'm picking beans.'

He buried his face in her shoulder. 'She's the Devil,' he murmured.

'Now, now, Andrew, she's your little friend.'

He looked at his mother earnestly. 'Never let her be you. She mustn't get in.'

The boy and girl have left the beach: she has led him into the most beautiful place in the world, where the sound of water dripping in solitary drops into a rock pool echoes off every facet of the vaulted chamber, and where the sunlight reflects in ripples across the rock ceiling.

She talks in a hushed voice. 'Isn't it lovely?'

'It's lovely,' he agrees. He likes her again, now.

'I discovered it, and no one else knows about it.'

He feels like her only friend. 'It's like heaven,' says the boy.

But she has to spoil everything. 'I don't believe in heaven,' she says.

The boy is upset. 'You have to!'

'I don't believe in hell either.'

'But you have to!'

'Why?'

' 'Cos . . . 'cos . . . when you die.'

'Huh.' She's contemptuous. 'When I die I shall rot away, like everyone else.'

It disturbs him, what she says. ' 'Tisn't like that!'

'And when I'm buried, wild dogs will come and dig up my grave and my ghost will come and haunt you!'

'No! No!' cries the boy.

But she climbs nimbly over the rocks towards the obscurity in the recesses of the cave. 'It's even better further in, it gets spooky.'

'Wait! Don't leave me alone,' he calls, fearfully. 'Joanne . . .! Joanne . . . ?'

His voice echoes unanswered.

Andrew looked up from where he sat on the sanctuary step. The vicar was standing quietly at the back.

'Vicar?' said Andrew. The vicar walked slowly up the aisle and stopped in front of him.

'Andrew, old chap,' he said.

'Don't let the bishop sign the paper,' said Andrew.

But it was not in the vicar's hands. He sat beside Andrew, and talked gently with him for about half an hour. Afterwards they both walked across to Andrew's house, where Millie had the kettle on.

The vicar and Millie chatted and drank their tea, while Andrew munched custard creams and pondered the vicar's earlier words. He didn't exactly understand what a psychological anxiety transference was, but the vicar, who knew about such things, had assured him that the Devil was not involved. Without wishing to get too technical (the vicar had said) it basically meant that Andrew had a fertile imagination, and though, goodness me, there was nothing wrong with imagination, no, it simply meant that these recent . . . worries had been caused by too much *thinking*. However, there were two things Andrew had to be completely clear about: firstly, there were no such things as ghosts (except the Holy Ghost, and that was something different), and secondly, even if there were, they couldn't possibly appear as another person. Categorically not.

Andrew took another custard cream. He felt curiously elated. It wasn't real, none of it was real. If he told it all to go away, it would. It was all in his head. All he had to do was say to himself, 'It's my imagination' (this was the vicar's suggestion), and it would disappear, pouff!

That evening Millie had a WI meeting. It was raining when she returned. She stamped her wet feet on the mat and shook her raincoat.

'Wet,' said Andrew, who had come to greet her in the hall.

'I don't know about locking the church,' she said, 'they should padlock the churchyard. Wretched animals.'

'What animals?' said Andrew.

'Scuffling, digging, scratching up the earth, never did like dogs. Shooed them off though. Mind out of the way, I'll have to change these shoes.'

Andrew froze. Wild dogs . . . When Millie had stomped upstairs, he tiptoed to the sitting-room window, lifted the corner of the curtain and looked churchwards. What a fool he'd been. Oh what a fool! He'd let himself be taken off guard, and now she was free, she was out. He could feel the numbness of terror taking hold inside his head.

He looked round the room. Here was obviously no longer safe: she would be coming for him any moment. The question was: could he make it to the church if he made a dash for it now, or would she be waiting for him to do just that, waiting in the darkness in the bushes beside the path? He took a deep breath and ran out of the house.

It was raining hard, but he scarcely noticed it. He opened the garden gate and lumbered out on to the church path. The bushes seemed full of menace, but he stared ahead of him as he ran, fixing his eyes on the south porch.

He reached the church, flung open the door, slammed it behind him and almost fell down the step. He knew the electricity was off, but he didn't need lights: not in here. He made his way forward to the front pew, and sat, relieved. He'd made it.

Now that the immediate panic was over, he made his plan. What he was going to do was this: he was going to spend all night here, and when they came with the padlock he'd take it away from them. Then he'd live here for ever. For ever.

The cave goes back a long way, narrowing, twisting and opening again into gloomy, chill places. The boy has followed the girl's voice into darkness, and now he has lost her.

'*Joanne. . .?*' *he asks.* '*Joanne . . .?*'

Her voice comes from where he did not expect it, some distance away. '*Here I am.*'

'*Where? I can't see you.*'

'*You should eat more carrots, and not so many sweets.*' *The voice seems to move about in the darkness.*

'*I'm going,*' *says the boy.* '*I hate you.*'

'*I thought you wanted to kiss me,*' *says the girl's voice, from somewhere else. He doesn't answer.* '*Don't you?*'

'*You're ugly,*' *he says.*

'*Not as ugly as you. You ought to be put down. We had a puppy once that was really ugly, and I drowned it. It was easy. I could drown you too, easy-peasy. Just leave you in here and wait for the tide to come in.*'

'*No you couldn't, you're not going to touch me. I'm going.*'

'*You don't know the way out, fatty.*'

'*Do!*' *he says. He hates her. He hates her.*

Instantly there is the sound of scrambling, and of falling stones, muddled with its own echo, then silence.

'*Joanne . . .?*' *says the boy, afraid.*

There is no sound, then, suddenly, close to his ear: '*Booh!*'

He lashes out, seizes what his hands find.

'*Ow, stop it, get off, stop it, Andrew!*' *She wrenches herself free and runs crunching across pebbles.* '*FatAndyfatAndyfatAndy fatAndyfatAndy . . .*'

He grabs whatever is at his feet—small stones, shingle— and flings it in fistfuls at the sound of the voice.

'*Don't! Stop it! Ow, Andrew! Don't!*'

He picks up bigger pebbles, flings them, panting, a constant barrage, not stopping, throwing indiscriminately, heavy stones, crying because he only wanted to be her friend.

'*Don't, Andrew, don't!*' *She's almost screaming.* '*Andrew, don't, don't, don't, don't. . .! Andrew! Andrew! Andr—*'

Her cries stop abruptly, but he does not seem to notice. He continues flinging stones, panting heavily. Then he turns and stumbles across the pebbles. He yells back to her: 'And I do know the way out. I do. I do!' And he is gone: returned to the sunlight and the sound of the sea breaking on the shore.

Andrew heard the church door open far behind him. He turned round. Torchlight bobbed.

'Andrew?' said his mother's voice.

'Mother,' said Andrew.

'What are you doing here?'

He could tell she was approaching, from the footsteps and the way the light moved. The footsteps came right up to him.

He thought. 'I came to look at the leak,' he said.

'At this time of night?' She turned and walked away towards the crypt stairway door.

Reluctantly, he got up and walked after the bobbing light.

She opened a door; listened. 'It's doing well.'

Andrew caught up. 'Sounds bad. Shine the torch.' But the stone stairs twisted out of sight.

'Down you go,' said Millie.

'We should get the vicar. We can't do anything.'

'Nonsense. On you go. You'll need your hands—I'll hold the torch.' She lit the first few steps for him.

'I don't like it, it's steep,' said Andrew. He reached the bend. 'Are you coming? You've got to come, Mother.' The light went out. 'Mother! What have you done? Turn it on!' There was no answer. 'I can't see!'

From the blackness at the top of the stone stairs came the soft voice that was not his mother's. 'You should eat more carrots and not so many sweets. I told you before.'

The chill went through him. 'Mother? Where are you?'

'She's not here,' said the soft voice. 'She's never been here.'

'She came in just now.'

'No,' said the voice. 'That was me.'

'You can't do that,' said Andrew. ''Tisn't possible. Vicar said.'

'The vicar!'

He tried the magic words. 'It was 'magination.'

'Shows how much he knows.'

'And it wasn't you last time, in the house. It was 'magination.'

'Oh yes, *that* was your imagination. But it was such a good idea I couldn't resist it. Do you mind?' The voice seemed to be coming closer, down the stairs, coming closer through the darkness, floating invisibly towards him. He backed down a step.

'You're not real,' he cried. 'You're not real! God, she's not here, tell her to go away! God?'

'He's not here either. He went this afternoon.' The voice was close now. 'Did you think He was staying till tomorrow?'

'You're not here, you're not here!'

The voice stopped an inch from his face. 'Don't you want to kiss me?'

Andrew leaned back from the touch of the long dead lips, slipped down a step. 'Don't come near me, leave me alone!'

But the voice was so close he could almost feel its breath. 'Kiss me . . .'

'No!' he cried. He lurched away from the terrible embrace, tripped, stumbled, lost balance, flung his hands out to save himself but grasped only air, and fell . . .

There were three inches of water in the crypt, but Andrew's head made a sharp crack as it hit the stone. He lay awkwardly, twisted, his legs half on the bottom steps, his face down. The water lapped his cheek. He didn't move.

Her feet nice and dry, Millie came downstairs. The front door was open again. 'Andrew?' she called, peering out into the rain from the doormat. 'Are you out there? What are you playing at?' No answer. She looked in the sitting-room, in the kitchen. Back at the front door, she called again: 'Andrew? I'm making some cocoa, I'm putting it on now. You know you don't like it with skin on.' That'll bring him if he's coming, she thought.

She pushed the door to and went to get the milk out of the fridge.

Somewhere else, the tide is coming in. A wave races foaming up the beach, across the rocks, and into a cave at the base of the cliff. A few moments later the water surges back through the pebbles to rejoin the sea and gather itself for the next wave. An hour later there is no cave to be seen.

When morning comes, the sea has retreated and the sun shines down once more. The rocks dry in the warmth of the new day.

Carlotta

ADÈLE GERAS

Diary of Edward Stonely, submitted in evidence at the Coroner's Inquest, 15 May 1993

My doctor (I refuse to call him 'my shrink', although that's what he is. It seems like an admission of madness.) has said that the dreams might stop altogether if I write everything down. It would be, he suggested, a kind of purging. It would clear my system of what he calls 'unresolved guilts.'

I felt a fool consulting him in the first place, but my dreams were becoming so dreadful that I was deliberately keeping myself awake for as long as I could every night. This meant that I was irritable and moody at school, tearing strips off both pupils and colleagues for no good reason. I was also horrible at home, to my wife Annie, whom I love more than anyone except my little daughter, Beth. I had not yet reached the point of taking my moods out on a four year old, but I can't have been the pleasantest dad in the world. The worst of it was, however hard I tried to stay awake, my eyelids closed in the end. They always did, every night, and every night, there she was: Carlotta.

'Start at the beginning,' Dr Armstrong said when I made some remark about not knowing where to begin. 'Don't leave anything out. Go on to the end of what you have to say and then stop. Write it as a kind of diary, whenever you feel you have something to say.' He made it sound so easy. Here goes:

19 November 1992
My name is Edward Stonely. I am thirty years old. I teach Art at St Peter's School in the small town of W . . . I'd rather not name it. I am good at what I do. I enjoy the teaching. When I left Art School, I had the mad idea that I might make a living from painting and sculpture, and took the job at the school just to make ends meet till I hit the big time.

That was seven years ago. The big time isn't something I think about any more, not really, though I do sometimes wish I had more time to give to my own work. As it is, I paint and sculpt mostly during the school holidays, and I'm happy to do so, because of Annie and Beth. I would be happy to do almost anything for them, in spite of everything. It's because I don't want to hurt them that I'm writing all this down, trying to get myself sorted out before it's too late.

I have a good job, a lovely wife and child, a house I can afford to pay for, a reasonable future. You would think, wouldn't you, that there was nothing left to wish for, but there is. I wish for peace. I wish I could be rid of Carlotta. There. I've written it down, so now maybe the blackness and solidity of the words will be like a magic spell to wipe my mind clean of those terrible dreams. I feel like Hamlet. I suppose you would say I identify with him, because of what happened to Carlotta, but we studied the play at school and I remember one quotation from it very well because I've thought it myself many times over the past few weeks. 'O God,' Hamlet says, 'I could be bounded in a nutshell and count myself a king of infinite space, were it not that I have bad dreams.' That's exactly what I think.

22 November

I can see it's pointless going any further without writing about Carlotta. I was in love with her for a year when I was seventeen, and she a little younger. She turned up at school one September, out of the blue, and the minute I saw her I knew she was different.

Plenty of other girls in the class were pretty, and I'd had my flirtations with quite a lot of them, kissing in the dark at the movies, or at discos, or parties, sighing a bit but not really suffering when the relationships came to a natural end. Good teenage fun. From the moment Carlotta arrived at school, everything altered for me. The other lads didn't rate her at all, so there wasn't much competition for her favours.

'Funny-looking,' my friend Geoff called her.

'Flat as a pancake,' said Marty, the class sexist pig.

'Silent, too,' said Pete, and their attitudes summed up what everyone thought about Carlotta except me. I could see that her thin body, and her strange, widely-spaced yellowy-green eyes in a somewhat flat face were not conventionally pretty, but they made my mouth dry whenever I looked at her, and my heart pounded when I passed close to her and smelled the wonderful fragrance that seemed to float about her hair.

Her hair . . . even Geoff and Marty and Pete agreed they had never seen anything like it. She wore it long and loose around her shoulders, and it waved and moved as she walked with a life of its own. Everyone called it black, but that was taking the easy way out. I spent hours staring at it, and there were blues and greens and even reds mixed up in the colour somehow, and a gleam on it as it caught the light.

I spent two weeks watching her at the beginning of that term, and then I could bear it no longer. Looking back, I can see that even the way our relationship started was odd. There was no leading up to it, no flirtation, no 'my friend fancies your friend' kind of negotiation that goes on in school romances.

We were in the Art Room, clearing up. There was no one else there. She was washing brushes in the sink. I came up behind her and buried my face in her hair. For a moment it felt as though I were drowning in the fragrance and the softness, and I prayed that I would never ever need to come up for air. She trembled, and then turned to face me.

Have you ever seen dry paper and wood flare up when you drop a lighted match on them? That's what happened to us. To Carlotta and me. Love had set us alight and we caught fire. We crackled and burned and leapt up in blinding flames of scarlet and gold. We were consumed.

For six months, everything seemed to disappear, and there were just the two of us and our passion in the whole world. And then (like a fire) the love on my part began to flicker a little, and dwindle and die. I'm not making excuses for myself. I know what I did was probably harsher than it need have been, but how was I to know that Carlotta would react as she did? I came to the conclusion that our relationship had to end, and I told her so. It happens all the time, doesn't it? Well, doesn't it? Don't boys and girls split up every day of the week with no harm done?

Carlotta seemed very calm when I told her. The yellow eyes widened. Her face turned quite white. She said a strange thing, one whose meaning I am only now beginning to understand:

'I'm not ready to let you go. Not yet. Not ever.'

Then she turned and left the room and that was the last time anyone saw her alive.

No one had an explanation for how she came to fall off the bridge over the rain-swollen river, with nobody seeing her, nor for why she should have died when we all knew she was a strong swimmer. One theory was that her hair had become entangled on some underwater obstacle as she fell, and that she was unable to free herself. No one else knew that I had ditched her hours before 'the accident'. No one else knew that Carlotta meant to die. Me and Hamlet. Neither of us guessed that love could be so strong, so unforgiving.

29 November
I grieved for Carlotta. Of course I did. I was genuinely sorry that she was dead. Of course I was, but I have to admit that a tiny part of me was furious with her. I can see, I said to myself, what she is saying: 'You killed me, Edward. You did. So suffer.' And I did suffer a bit, but I got over it. I went to Art School. I met Annie. We fell in love and married. Beth was born. I hardly ever thought about Carlotta. Then a few months ago, the dreams started. Dr Armstrong said:

'Tell me what happens in these dreams. Why they are so dreadful.'

'They don't sound dreadful when I tell them,' I said. 'It's Carlotta speaking. Just her head floating in water, with her hair drifting backwards and forwards like seaweed. She says: I'm coming. I haven't forgotten. I'll be there soon. Very soon, and then we'll be together for ever. I shall touch you, she says and then she stretches out two hands in front of her and they're all bones and fragments of skin and I know that if I don't wake up now she will clutch me in her hideous fingers.'

'Hmm,' Dr Armstrong said. 'How very unpleasant. You clearly still feel responsible for Carlotta's unfortunate accident . . . still perceive it as suicide. Have you tried painting a picture of her? Or perhaps making a clay model . . . Maybe that would help . . . giving your nightmares a real, physical presence.'

I promised Dr Armstrong that I would try.

10 February 1993

I haven't written in this notebook for some weeks. I think I may be cured. I have much to be grateful to Dr Armstrong for. The dreams have almost completely left me. Just before Christmas, I started work on a series of paintings I call 'Portraits of Carlotta'. Annie (who knows everything) tried to pretend she didn't mind that I was spending every moment when I was not at school 'locked up in the studio with another woman', as she put it.

All through the Christmas holidays I slaved over my canvases. There are enough here for an exhibition, but I am reluctant to let anyone see them. Carlotta's yellow eyes follow me wherever I go. There's one portrait in particular I'm pleased with, where she seems almost to be walking out of the frame and into the room. She has her hands held out in front of her like a sleepwalker. Sometimes, I find myself wanting to touch her, and I put my hands out so that they almost reach the hands in the painting.

20 February

How am I going to write this? I pray that my darling Annie will never read it. But I have to say it. If I put it down on paper, it may not be so dangerous. If I don't say it, I feel the strength of my own feelings may cause me to explode. A strange thing happened last night. I had nearly finished another portrait of Carlotta: a close-up of her face taking up almost the entire canvas. I was painting the half-open mouth when suddenly I found that the brush had fallen out of my hand and my own lips were touching Carlotta's. I was kissing her image. This was bad enough. Worse, oh, so much worse, was what I was experiencing as my mouth came into contact with cold paint. I was as stirred by this lifeless kiss as I had been the first time I had kissed the real Carlotta, all those years ago in the Art Room.

I tore myself away from the painting, and went to lie on the studio sofa, feeling sick, and hot, as though some dreadful fever had seized hold of me. I feel somewhat calmer now, writing this away from the studio, where she can't see me, but now that I am calmer, I can face the truth. She has enchanted me all over again. I want her. I wish we could be together once again. I think she has driven me mad.

Yesterday I found myself looking at her outstretched hands in the portrait I like best of all. The perspective has worked, I thought. She really does look as though she is about to walk out of the frame. I put my hands out and touched her painted ones. This must be what an electric shock feels like, I thought. I must stop. I must stop this madness now before it's too late. Oh, Carlotta, I am longing, hurting, burning for you! I cannot bear it.

10 April

The exhibition is over. It was an enormous success. Every single one of the portraits has been sold. The local paper called the show 'a moving tribute by one of her old schoolfriends to the tragic victim of a drowning accident'. I am a celebrity at school. Annie, I can see, is mightily relieved to have the canvases out of the house. I am bereft. I cannot live without her. I shall make her again. Differently this time. I shall take clay and fashion her once more. I shall paint the clay in all the colours of her skin and hair . . . bring her to some kind of life. I shall tell no one at all about this. It will be our secret. Carlotta's and mine.

1 May

It is done. Now we can be together. Carlotta, fetch me. Take me with you.

* * *

3 May 1993 Extract from the statement of Mrs Anne Stonely, submitted in evidence at the Coroner's Inquest

Beth was fast asleep in her room. We always had our supper, Edward and I, after she had gone to bed. I called him to come and eat, but he didn't come, so I went to find him. There was nothing strange about this. He often became so absorbed in his work that he lost all track of time and place.

I went into the studio. I hadn't been in there for ages. I didn't know he had begun to work in clay. As soon as I saw him, slumped like that against the model of a woman, I knew he was dead. His legs were trailing on the floor. Her arms were around him. It was almost as if she were holding him up. His head was thrown back. The woman's head had lolled forward. It was horrible. They were tangled up together. The worst thing of all was the hair. Her hair seemed to be filling his mouth. It almost looked as though he were eating it. I became hysterical. I knew who she was supposed to be. I recognized the long black hair. It was Carlotta. I ran out of the studio screaming and my neighbour heard me, and phoned the police and our family doctor, Dr Cooper.

Later, Dr Cooper told me what he had found. I can't understand it. Edward, it seems, had choked to death, even though they had no idea at all of what might have choked him. There was no sign at all of anyone else having been in the studio, although the floor was awash with water. No one knew where this had come from. Neither Dr Cooper nor the police could find any sign of a woman fashioned out of clay. They took me to the studio to show me, and I couldn't see her either. Not any more.

Dr Cooper says I must have become hysterical when I discovered Edward lying there dead, and imagined the whole thing. I must have. I hope that I did. Otherwise, what happened, and where Carlotta is now, are too horrible even to think about.

Little Black Pies

JOHN GORDON

Ghosts,' she said. 'There ain't no such thing.'

Emma Stittle watched her plump arm spread and become fatter as she pressed it on the kitchen table.

'There ain't no such thing,' she repeated, and with her thumb stripped peas from a pod, cupped them in the palm of her hand and raised them to her mouth. 'Ghosts is a load of old squit.'

Her sister Sarah, thinner and older, rattled the poker between the bars of the kitchen stove, and red coals and ashes fell into the grate. 'It get so hot in this kitchen on a summer's day,' she said, 'that I wonder I bother to cook anything at all.'

'Me,' said Emma, 'I reckon it's stupid to think that people who eat can die and then turn into somethin' that don't need food.' She chewed as she slit another pod with her thumbnail. 'I like peas, but there ain't no substance in 'em.'

Sarah had no time to talk of ghosts. 'I'm that hot I

don't know what to do with myself,' she said as she hobbled towards the cottage door, narrow-shouldered and stooping. She lifted the latch and pulled the door open. 'Come you on in then,' she said. 'All on you, you little black devils.' A great ramp of sunlight streamed through the door to brighten the tiled floor. 'Flies,' she said, 'swarms on 'em.'

There was a dance of black specks above Emma's head but she paid no heed. 'When our old mother used to talk of ghosts,' she said, 'she used to make me frit. She used to say they come back because their time weren't properly run. That there was unfinished business or somethin' like that. Load of old squit.'

'Who does all the work round here? Who?' Sarah, like her sister, wore a flowered, wrap-around apron, and both had their hair drawn back into buns, but Sarah's hair was grey while her sister's was still glossy black. 'I scrimp and save and slave and scrub,' she said, coming back to the table, 'and what thanks did I ever get for it? She died, didn't she? And never no word of thanks. Not one.' She banged an earthenware bowl on to the bare wood of the table in front of Emma and began scooping flour into it from a big jar.

Emma sat where she was, her round cheeks dimpling as she munched. 'You look a bit wore up today, Sarah,' she said. 'What's been gettin' you down, gal?'

Sarah cut a wedge of lard and began rubbing it into the flour with her skinny brown fingers. 'I slaved all o' them years after Father died and Mother was left alone. I skivvied from morning till night and what help did I get?' She dug savagely into the white mess.

'I were much younger than you, Sarah, don't forget. Only a little kid when Mother were taken poorly. And I used to sit beside her up in her room and keep her company hour after hour.'

Sarah did not look her way. Her blue eyes, fading with age, gazed at where her fingers dug. 'Spoilt brat.' The wrinkles of her thin face arranged themselves into a simper and her voice took on an acid whine. 'Please, Sarah, Mummy's sent me down for a cup of tea. I'll take it up, Sarah. Mummy don't want nobody else to disturb her.'

'I weren't ever as bad as that. You're putting it on.' Emma was laughing. 'But she did like me to sit with her. She used to sit in that old high-backed chair by the window, with her shawl around her, and her pillows, and I used to pull aside the lace curtain so as we could see down into the lane, and she used to tell me things about everybody that came by.' Emma chewed and laughed again. 'She told me things no kid ought never to have been told. About women in the village. And men.'

Sarah paid her no attention. She poured a little water from a jug into the basin and mixed it in with a knife, jabbing. 'Best frock. Always best frock because, ''Mummy likes to see me pretty.'' And who done the scrubbing with a sack tied round her waist? Who took out the ashes and blackleaded the stove? Twice a week I done that, and all the cracks in the skin o' me fingers shown up like black spider webs.'

But Emma was in a reverie. She gazed through the open door across the lane to where the yew trees shaped themselves against the blue sky. 'She used to love a funeral. Especially if they dug the grave near enough so she could see the coffin go down. She used to love telling me how people died. Little Claudie Copp called for his Mum all through one night, she say, and he never once

49

see her alongside his bed. And then in the morning, Mother used to say, he went up to heaven with the angels.'

'Like black spider webs.' Sarah slashed the dough across and lifted half of it on to a piece of oilcloth where she had sprinkled flour. 'I could've had nice hands. Nice soft white hands like I seen some girls have, but they was always in water. Always scrubbing.'

'It was lucky for her we lived just across from the churchyard,' said Emma. 'Gave her an interest. People always visitin' graveyards. And stayin' there in the end.' She laughed again and looked towards her sister, but Sarah had a new grievance.

'I could've had him if I wasn't so thin and dry and wore out with work. I could've.' She rubbed flour on to the rolling pin and began to roll out the dough. 'I had his child, didn't I?' The pastry was a thin white island on the oilcloth. 'I had his little baby.' A tear came from the inner corner of one faded eye, but was so thin it did no more than moisten the side of her nose.

'You never did!' Emma's eyes gleamed with surprise and curiosity. 'Whose baby? You never said nothing. I never seen no baby.'

Sarah had turned her back to get a pie dish from the window ledge. 'I never told nobody. Nobody ever knew.'

'But who was he, Sarah? I never knew you had a feller.' Her sister remained silent, and Emma became sly. 'I don't mean you never had admirers. I used to think my Tom looked at you a bit. Used to, till I made him stop.'

Sarah lifted the pastry and began to line the pie dish. 'Tom were a lovely man.' The glisten of a tear came and went. 'He were lovely.'

'So I were right.' Emma turned her plump face away

and patted the glossy bun at the back of her head. 'I guessed as much. Tom never said nothing but I guessed as much.'

'If I'd told him about the child he would have married me. I know that. But I could never hold a man because of that—not when his eyes was on my own sister.'

Emma had jerked towards her, her mouth open, but Sarah's voice did not change its pitch.

'So I lost him, didn't I?' She had lifted the pie dish and was trimming the pastry at the edge. 'And there was nothing but the baby.'

'Tom's baby.' Emma's whisper was as soft as the ash that fell in the grate.

'It died,' said Sarah. 'I made it die. And it lies yonder still, under that tree. No father, no mother, nothing.'

Emma's round face was pinched suddenly and her voice was harsh and vindictive. 'It's as well for you there ain't no such thing as ghosts, Sarah Stittle, or else you would be haunted!'

But Sarah spoke as though Emma was not there. 'First she took Mother from me, then she took Tom, and I never said a word. Never said, and I ought to have done. I ought to have said.'

Emma opened her mouth to speak, but a sudden flutter of wings in the doorway made both sisters start. A jackdaw, twisting his grey nape in the sunshine, stood on the step.

Emma gasped. 'My God, that were like the angel o' death. That whole doorway seemed full of black wings. I can't stand birds. I hate them stiff feathers. Go away! Get out, you devil of hell!'

But Sarah was wiping her hands on her apron as she went towards the doorway. Her face softened with pleasure. 'Come on then, my beauty. Come you on in and see your Auntie Sarie. There now, there now.' She stooped and held out a finger. The bird hopped on it. 'Lovely little cold black claws you've got, my lovely boy. Hold tight to your auntie.'

'Take it away! Take it away!' Emma shrank back in her chair. 'Please, Sarah!'

But Sarah spoke only to the bird. 'You came when I needed you, my lovely. You came hopping over the road just when I were down in the dumps, my lovely boy.' She raised the bird and her dry lips touched his black bill.

'Sarah! I can't bear it!'

'Just when I needed you, you came hopping along with your black eye. And didn't you know it all, didn't you just know it?' For the first time, the bird against her cheek, its black feathers touching her grey hair, she looked directly towards her sister. 'Emma took my man, didn't she? Emma took my man. But you showed me, didn't you, boy? You showed me how he'd never have her. Never no more. Skippety along the lane, skippety down the hollow. You showed me the pretty flower and the little black berry. The little black berry I put in the pie. One, two, three . . . many, many more. In a little pie for Emma. Emma's little pie.'

'You're talking daft, Sarah. What you on about? Throw that bird out. Get rid of it.'

'And Emma never knew.' Sarah sat and stroked the bird, looking no more towards her sister. 'Emma never knew about them little black berries what she ate. Ate many and many a time.'

'My stomach,' said Emma. 'I had a bad stomach and you gave me little pies to ease it. They was nice.' She tried to smile, but although the dimples came they were pale.

'I gave her pies, my beauty. Little black pies. And now she ain't got no stomach-ache no more. Nothing no more.'

Emma made herself laugh. 'Sarah!' she called. 'Sarah, look at me!' But Sarah did not stir. 'Sarah, you make me feel bad. What did you do to me?'

Sarah held the bird so her nose was touching its deep grey cap. 'I wish we could tell her what we done, Jack my beauty. I wish we could tell her, but it's too late now.'

'What do you mean too late? What you done to me?'

But Sarah ignored her sister's cry, kissed the bird and put it down on the table. 'You like to peck peas, Jack. There you are, my little boy, my lovey. Go you peck them peas.'

The fat woman pressed her arm on the table and clenched her fist on the peas.

'You ain't going to scare me,' she said. 'You ain't going to scare me with your talk. You talk as if I was dead. But if I was, how come I'm here?' She laughed, defying her sister. 'There ain't no such thing as ghosts.'

The bird's black claws skittered on the table top as it went towards the clenched fist. Emma clutched tight, refusing to move. The bird stabbed down. She clutched tighter and shrieked. But the room was silent. And the black beak pecked through a hand that nobody but Emma herself could see.

53

The Guitarist

GRACE HALLWORTH

Joe was always in demand for the Singings, or community evenings held in villages which were too far away from the city to enjoy its attractions. He was an excellent guitarist and when he wasn't performing on his own, he accompanied the singers and dancers who also attended the Singing.

After a Singing someone was sure to offer Joe a lift back to his village but on one occasion he found himself stranded miles away from his home with no choice but to set out on foot. It was a dark night and there wasn't a soul to be seen on the road, not even a cat or a dog, so Joe began to strum his guitar to hearten himself for the lonely journey ahead.

Joe had heard many stories about strange things seen at night on that road but he told himself that most of the people who related these stories had been drinking heavily. All the same, as he came to a crossroad known to be the haunt of Lajables and other restless spirits, he strummed his guitar loudly to drown the rising clamour of fearful thoughts in his head. In the quiet of early morning the tune was sharp and strong, and Joe began to move to the rhythm; but all the while his eyes were fixed on a point ahead of him where four roads met. The nearer he got, the more convinced he was that someone was standing in the middle of the road. He hoped with all his heart that he was wrong and that the shape was only a shadow cast by an overhanging tree.

The man stood so still he might have been a statue, and it was only when Joe was within arm's length of the figure that he saw any sign of life. The man was quite tall, and so thin that his clothes hung on him as though they were thrown over a wire frame. There was a musty smell about them. It was too dark to see who the man was or what he looked like, and when he spoke his voice had a rasp to it which set Joe's teeth on edge.

'You play a real fine guitar for a youngster,' said the man, falling into step beside Joe.

Just a little while before, Joe would have given anything to meet another human being but somehow he was not keen to have this man as a companion. Nevertheless his motto was 'Better to be safe than sorry' so he was as polite as his unease would allow.

'It's nothing special, but I like to keep my hand in. What about you, man? Can you play guitar too?' asked Joe.

'Let me try your guitar and we'll see if I can match you,' replied the man. Joe handed over his guitar and the man began to play so gently and softly that Joe had to listen closely to hear the tune. He had never heard such a mournful air. But soon the music changed, the tune became wild and the rhythm fast and there was a harshness about it which drew a response from every nerve in Joe's body. Suddenly there was a new tone and mood and the music became light and enchanting. Joe felt as if he were borne in the air like a blown-up balloon. He was floating on a current of music and would follow it to the ends of the earth and beyond.

And then the music stopped. Joe came down to earth with a shock as he realized that he was standing in front of his house. The night clouds were slowly dispersing. The man handed the guitar back to Joe who was still dazed.

'Man, that was guitar music like I never heard in this world before,' said Joe.

'True?' said the man. 'You should have heard me when I was alive!'

The Chocolate Ghost

JULIA HAWKES-MOORE

The friends Kate and Sarah made chocolates. In fact, they looked rather like the chocolates which they made. Both girls were very large, tall and wide, plump and bosomy, with skins as glossy as cocoa butter. Their long shining hair was swept up with ribbons tied on top. They wore frilly aprons with lacy petticoats peeping out like decorative doilies under the hems of their flounced skirts.

Kate's hair was plain-chocolate dark and Sarah was milky-blonde. Kate was as tough as Brazil nuts beneath her crispy outer shell, whilst Sarah was sugar sweet right through to her soft centre. Their smiles were as toothy and welcoming as those on their Easter white chocolate bunnies, and they were altogether as delightful as the luscious plains, milks, and fudges which they made each week.

The chocolate girls decided to buy a shop. They only had a little money, so they had to hunt around for a long time before they found somewhere cheap and pretty enough to suit their purpose.

In a little cobbled street just off the market square they found a tall, narrow house squeezed in between two strict Georgian red-brick ones. It was all tottery with carved oak beams, and diamondy window-panes. It was cheap because it had been empty for many years and the pre-war paint had all peeled away. It had once been a sweetshop, but no one had wanted to move into it, because it was rumoured to be haunted.

Certainly the place had an atmosphere, which very slightly raised the hair on the back of their necks as the girls walked around with the estate agent. But nothing could bother the chocolate girls. Merry, practical spirits, they shook hands on the agreement then and there, tripping gaily away to sign the deeds.

Surprisingly soon they were back, proud as princesses of their new realm. They whooped for joy as the door swung open to their key, and danced in the dust. They attacked the huge task with gusto, and half-filled their hired skip with debris before darkness fell on their first day of ownership.

Tired and filthy, they slammed the front door with a happy thud. Gazing up at the scruffy but pretty building which was now theirs, their eyes caught a slight movement in the topmost window. It looked for a moment as though a body swung by its neck behind the cobwebbed panes.

'Trick of the light,' Kate decided, and they sauntered away.

Next morning, they were back early to start again. To their surprise, the neatly stacked brooms, mops, and pails lay sprawled across the floor.

'We must stop slamming that door!' laughed Kate, and they picked up all the things and went back to work.

At last the shop was hygienic and sparkling, and they decorated it in rich milky creams and toothsome dark chocolate browns. It was all frilled with sweeping curtains, lacy nets, and golden ribbons, the entire shop a beautiful box in which to display their finest chocolates. There was a grand opening, involving the Mayor and Mayoress, champagne and rum truffles. The gleaming old inlaid brass cash register was soon tinkling merrily with the chocolate girls' incomes.

Yet as Sarah worked, she became increasingly aware of the feeling of being watched; but every time she turned around sharply, she saw nothing but shadows.

Late that evening, Kate studied Sarah's frowning face under her fluffy blonde fringe. 'It's not like you to get so worried about something, Sarah. What is it?'

'Kate, you don't suppose that there's a ghost in the shop, do you? It's just that I'm starting to get the feeling that we're not very welcome. There is something nasty here, I don't know what. But I do know that it doesn't like us one bit. I feel . . . scared of it.' Sarah blushed foolishly under her friend's stare. 'Just forget it, I'm talking nonsense.'

Kate continued to look at her silently. Although she was unwilling to admit it, she too had become gradually aware of small sounds, of flickers of movement in the corner of her eye, and the hair stirred on the back of her neck. She reached up to rub the suddenly aching muscles of her shoulders, and yawned.

'Ghosts, indeed! I don't know about any daft old ghosts. All I know about is making chocolates, and we've got a week's supply of cream truffles to make tomorrow morning. We're just overtired after all our hard work. Tell you what, let's go down to the Three Crowns tomorrow night; there's a good band on. We'll get all tarted up, and check out the talent, hey? It's about time we treated ourselves to a good flirt with some dishy fellas!'

Sarah giggled at her suggestion; 'Will do!' she cried. 'I'll wear my new red Lycra dress. Now go and get some sleep, Kate; you look ready to drop.'

Kate yawned again, and turned away. She began to climb the stairs slowly and heavily, watching her feet on the narrow steps. Sarah glanced up towards Kate's bedroom door, then froze in horror. She let out a shriek:

'Kate! Behind you, Kate, look!'

Kate glanced up the last few stairs and cried out in disbelief. Staring down at her, just inches in front of her own face, was the wild-eyed and vicious face of an old man. His hair stood out in an unkempt and greying shock, his stained teeth were bared in a wide snarl. Although his form was smoky and insubstantial, Kate, rigid with fear, felt the clutch of his pincer-like fingers on her shoulders, and tried to scream out for help as he spun her round, then gave her a mighty shove. The scream only began to spill out of her open mouth as she fell headlong down the steep staircase. She stretched out her arms, trying desperately to slow her heavy fall.

Sarah rushed forward to catch her friend as she reached the bottom of the stairs, and the two girls collapsed in a heap. As her knees buckled beneath Kate's weight, Sarah glanced upwards, only to see a smoky haze fading away into nothing, but leaving the distinct impression of a leering face, laughing down at the disaster below.

Kate moaned, stirred and burst into tears, Sarah joining her a split-second later, as she helped Kate to uncoil and straighten up. Then Sarah flung her arms around Kate's neck, and they both cried and cried. The horror of the hideous face which they had both seen, the shock of Kate's fall, and the tensions and worries of the last few weeks all flooded out, until their hair and faces were wet and their eyelids swollen.

At last, all cried-out, the girls separated, to catch their breath and look at each other, wide-eyed with disbelief at the situation. They each glanced back upstairs, but Kate shook her head fiercely.

'No way am I staying here tonight. You can, if you like, but I'm not going up those stairs again in a hurry. I'm going back to my parents' place tonight. Get your stuff, if you want to come with me.' Kate's words were clear, but her voice shook with emotion.

Sarah nodded, and hurried to collect her coat and bag, then they carefully descended the next flight of stairs into the shop. They glanced around, sadly, at the display of hard work and hope which they had put into the shop, both sighing. Then they unlocked the shop door, closing it gently behind them.

'Burglars?' Sarah enquired tearfully, the next morning, as the girls gazed around them at the debris of a once-lovely sweet shop.

The glass shelves of beribboned boxes of hand-made chocolates had been swept clear, and all those pretty things lay squashed and mangled on the floor.

Kate pointed at the walls, jabbing her finger at the ugly scrawls of loopy writing, smeared across the creamy paintwork. 'What about all that?' she demanded. 'Obscenities and filthy suggestions. Not what we want our customers to read. No, Sarah, that's not burglars, not with twenty quid still in the till, and none of the selection boxes missing. That's the flipping supernatural. You were right. We are haunted.'

'Can we get it exorcised?' Sarah sobbed.

Kate drew a deep breath. Thrusting a tissue into Sarah's hand, she declared, 'Right! Let's go and see that snooty estate agent who sold us the shop. We'll sort this out!'

The estate agent, confronted by Kate, sighed, and told them the story of the haunted sweetshop.

Long ago, it had been bought by a young man called Jim Evans. He had planned to share it as a new home and business with his fiancée. She was a pretty little thing, all pouts and ringletty curls, and with a very sweet tooth. Jim courted her with barley sugar, pressed her with candyfloss, and finally won her hand with a bagful of marrons glacés. Tragically, the war broke out during their gentle and sticky courtship, and sugar rationing ruined his hopes. He bribed her with sugared almonds for kisses, and then he couldn't supply enough sugared almonds.

She resisted his increasingly shabby advances throughout the war, until all that he could offer was the promise of marzipan on their dried-egg wedding cake. She jilted him when he confessed that he could not afford the icing-sugar, and then she ran off with an American GI, who enticed her with unlimited Hershey bars.

Her abandoned lover hardened his heart against all women, with the ferocity of boiling toffee. He short-measured any female over the age of nine (or younger if they wore ringlets), and was so surly to the mothers and grandmothers of his little customers that his trade fell slowly but surely away.

Eventually, Jim Evans found himself without any

income or friends, unable to pay his rates demands, and heartbroken, all because of that long-lost young lady with a sweet tooth.

One dark night, Jim took a rope and hanged himself in his bedroom, but his body spun there slowly, undiscovered for days. No one attended the funeral.

'What a sad, sad story,' whispered Sarah, as they trudged home. 'No wonder Jim Evans hated us young women moving into his house and selling sweets in his shop. It makes me want to help him in some way, not just banish the poor man . . . '

Kate regarded her thoughtfully. 'Jim Evans didn't just sell sweets, either—he used to make his own sweets like we make our own chocolates, and jolly good they were, too, that estate agent said. You can't get those flavours today . . . '

'I beg your pardon,' said Sarah indignantly, wiping away her tears. 'It's the big businesses that have changed all the techniques, but you and I can recapture the old taste of sweets, you know, because we work on such a small scale. It's just the recipes that are hard to find.'

Kate turned to look at her in surprise. Sarah pointed to the scrawls on the wall. 'And if Jim Evans can write rude words—even if he can't spell them—then he could write his recipes down as well. We could do a deal with him.'

'Are you suggesting that if we don't exorcize him, he might give us his recipes?'

Sarah's eyes were gleaming, as she seized Kate's hand; 'Kate, don't you see? He doesn't mind us selling sweets here, but he gets upset whenever we talk about meeting men. He's jealous and frightened because we might run away with other men, like his fiancée did. But if we work very hard, as we ought to, setting up a new business, then he's on our side. He could be a sort of sleeping partner, helping to build up the business of his dreams. But we must be faithful to him, if he's going to give us his precious recipes. I will, anyway! I want to make a go of this business. What about you, Kate?'

Kate stared. 'You're right, Sarah. I'll do it.' She shouted into the air: 'Jim Evans, we're the girls for you! Here's the deal. You give us your recipes, we'll sell them. And we'll be good girls. We'll look after you, if you look after us.' She started to laugh, and, grinning, sprang over to the gilt-edged blackboard where the flavour and price of the weekly special truffles were chalked up, and wiped it clear with her sleeve. She rested a small stick of chalk against it, and stepped back.

Then she grabbed Sarah by the wrist, pushed her into the kitchen at the back of the shop, and firmly closed the door behind them both.

'Now,' she declared, 'we give him his chance. Sarah, the broom. Let's start tidying up in here—we've got a business to run.' She grabbed the mop, and started feverishly washing down the walls.

The kitchen was restored to sanity and hygiene long before they dared to venture back into the shop. Everything was as disordered and tangled as before. With great trepidation, they tiptoed over the carpet of squashed sweets towards the blackboard, and peered at it in disbelief.

Covering its surface with close-written, misspelled writing was a recipe.

'Crystallized flowerpetals,' Sarah read aloud. 'Jim is sorry; he does want to help. And he's giving us bouquets of flowers to apologize, in the only way he knows how.

Oh, you sweetie-pie!' she trilled to the empty air. 'Thank you. We'll make them at once. They'll sell really well, won't they, Kate?' She pirouetted around to look into the face of her friend, her eyes alight with hope.

Kate regarded her silently, and bit her lip as she considered. 'Well,' she mused aloud, 'we could try making them this evening, instead of going to that dance, to see if the recipe really works.'

Sarah clapped her hands in glee. 'Yes. Oh, you lovely man, Jim Evans!' she shouted triumphantly into the air. 'This could be the start of something really special, don't you think, Kate?'

Kate smiled and hugged her friend. Both girls then turned and began restoring the shop to order.

Soon, the sugar-kettles in the kitchen simmered and steamed, and the air was treacly and fragrant with flowers and caramel. Kate plucked petals into china basins. Sarah dipped and dried and carefully arranged.

The completed articles were enchanting. The boxes were laid out in formal swirls and lozenges like the knot-gardens of medieval manor-houses. Strips of succulent green angelica were interwoven with lengths of barley-sugar around panels of delicate rose-petals, vivid marigolds, and fragile preserved violets. Stepping-stones of crystallized ginger lay across pools of blue candied lavender buds. Little mounds of sugared coffee beans appeared like tiny rockeries, garlanded with pearls of coriander seed and fronds of maidenhair fern, frozen beneath a crackling glaze of syrup.

Made with love and lavished with attention, these confections were bought as soon as they appeared for sale. The shop became so busy that they had to expand the shop-space into the kitchens, and hire workshops in a nearby village.

Jim Evans seemed to have repented fully of his cruelty to the chocolate girls when they first opened their shop in his home. For Jim Evans, failure, outcast, and reject of society as he had been, to have the world rushing to his door to buy his confectionery pleased him deeply. The atmosphere of gloom within the house had evaporated in the bubbly, frilly and merry charm of success which seemed to bless every new venture of the chocolate girls' business empire. Kate and Sarah greeted Jim with thanks each morning, as a new recipe appeared. They wished him farewell each night, leaving out samples of the new sweets, which had always vanished by dawn.

The public bought the sweets, and were consumed by memories. For elderly people, a single cachou or parma violet brought images of lost and beloved childhood faces. Younger people explored the mysteries of jujubes, lozenges, liquorice laces, and aniseed balls. Tigernuts, Spanish tobacco, bulls' eyes, and sherbet suckers were bought by the pound, whilst jamboree bags with all their hidden surprises proved very popular. Love-letters and satin cushions were exchanged by lovers as frequently as were the original truffles and hand-made chocolates which Kate and Sarah still produced.

At last the morning dawned when Jim had no more recipes to leave for his chocolate girls. His repertoire was exhausted, even to its last sugar mouse. Ready for work, the girls descended to find a tender farewell blessing chalked onto the blackboard, signed with two large wavering kisses. As they stood still in surprise before the board, they each felt the touch of a hand laid gently on their shoulders. Turning slowly, Kate and Sarah looked into the sadly smiling face of an old grey man standing silently behind them. He leaned forward, wisping a kiss over the cheek of each girl, softly as a cobweb. Then the ghost of Jim Evans faded away for ever.

Sarah wept copiously, and even Kate had to brush away several tears. They hugged each other to comfort their sudden sense of loss.

The shop seemed bigger and quieter without Jim, and the future seemed blander. But not for long.

Sarah wiped her eyes and gazed up at Kate. A slow, curling smile broke across her tear-streaked face, and her wet eyes gleamed in excitement. 'Well, Kate, now that Jim has left the shop, you know what we can do at last, don't you?'

Kate looked at her, and a beaming smile gradually lit up her features. 'Yes, of course! Now we can really start to live—it's been all work and no play for quite long enough, eh, Sarah? We've been very good for a long time, haven't we? Now let's start celebrating our success, by going to a dance!'

As for the generous spirit who had inspired and dictated their success, Kate and Sarah immortalized him in the name of their traditional confectionery company: *The Chocolate Ghost*.

The Haunted Mill

JEROME K. JEROME

Well, you all know my brother-in-law, Mr Parkins (began Mr Coombes, taking the long clay pipe from his mouth, and putting it behind his ear; we did not know his brother-in-law, but we said we did, so as to save time), and you know of course that he once took a lease of an old mill in Surrey, and went to live there.

Now you must know that, years ago, this very mill had been occupied by a wicked old miser, who died there, leaving—so it was rumoured—all his money hidden somewhere about the place. Naturally enough, everyone who had since come to live at the mill had tried to find the treasure; but none had ever succeeded, and the local wiseacres said that nobody ever would, unless the ghost of the miserly miller should, one day, take a fancy to one of the tenants, and disclose to him the secret of the hiding-place.

My brother-in-law did not attach much importance to the story, regarding it as an old woman's tale, and, unlike

68

his predecessors, made no attempt whatever to discover the hidden gold.

'Unless business was very different then from what it is now,' said my brother-in-law, 'I don't see how a miller could very well have saved anything, however much a miser he might have been: at all events, not enough to make it worth the trouble of looking for it.'

Still, he could not altogether get rid of the idea of that treasure.

One night he went to bed. There was nothing very extraordinary about that, I admit. He often did go to bed of a night. What *was* remarkable, however, was that exactly as the clock of the village church chimed the last stroke of twelve, my brother-in-law woke up with a start, and felt himself quite unable to go to sleep again.

Joe (his Christian name was Joe) sat up in bed, and looked around.

At the foot of the bed something stood very still, wrapped in shadow.

It moved into the moonlight, and then my brother-in-law saw that it was a figure of a wizened little old man, in knee-breeches and a pig-tail.

In an instant the story of the hidden treasure and the old miser flashed across his mind.

'He's come to show me where it's hid,' thought my brother-in-law; and he resolved that he would not spend all this money on himself, but would devote a small percentage of it towards doing good to others.

The apparition moved towards the door: my brother-in-law put on his trousers and followed it. The ghost went downstairs into the kitchen, glided over and stood in front of the hearth, sighed and disappeared.

Next morning, Joe had a couple of bricklayers in, and made them haul out the stove and pull down the chimney, while he stood behind with a potato-sack in which to put the gold.

They knocked down half the wall, and never found so much as a four-penny bit. My brother-in-law did not know what to think.

The next night the old man appeared again, and again led the way into the kitchen. This time, however, instead of going to the fireplace, it stood more in the middle of the room, and sighed there.

'Oh, I see what he means now,' said my brother-in-law to himself; 'it's under the floor. Why did the old idiot go and stand up against the stove, so as to make me think it was up the chimney?'

They spent the next day in taking up the kitchen floor; but the only thing they found was a three-pronged fork, and the handle of that was broken.

On the third night, the ghost reappeared, quite unabashed, and for a third time made for the kitchen. Arrived there, it looked up at the ceiling and vanished.

'Umph! he don't seem to have learned much sense where he's been to,' muttered Joe, as he trotted back to bed; 'I should have thought he might have done that first.'

Still, there seemed no doubt now where the treasure lay, and the first thing after breakfast they started pulling down the ceiling. They got every inch of the ceiling down, and they took up the boards of the room above.

They discovered about as much treasure as you would expect to find in an empty quart-pot.

On the fourth night, when the ghost appeared, as usual, my brother-in-law was so wild that he threw his boots at it; and the boots passed through the body, and broke a looking-glass.

On the fifth night, when Joe awoke, as he always did now at twelve, the ghost was standing in a dejected attitude, looking very miserable. There was an appealing look in its large sad eyes that quite touched my brother-in-law.

'After all,' he thought, 'perhaps the silly chap's doing his best. Maybe he has forgotten where he really did put it, and is trying to remember. I'll give him another chance.'

The ghost appeared grateful and delighted at seeing Joe prepare to follow him, and led the way into the attic, pointed to the ceiling, and vanished.

'Well, he's hit it this time, I do hope,' said my brother-in-law; and next day they set to work to take the roof off the place.

It took them three days to get the roof thoroughly off, and all they found was a bird's nest; after securing which they covered up the house with tarpaulins, to keep it dry.

You might have thought that would have cured the poor fellow of looking for treasure. But it didn't.

He said there must be something in it all, or the ghost would never keep coming as it did; and that, having gone so far, he would go on to the end, and solve the mystery, cost what it might.

Night after night, he would get out of his bed and follow that spectral old fraud about the house. Each night, the old man would indicate a different place; and, on each following day, my brother-in-law would proceed to break up the mill at the point indicated, and look for the treasure. At the end of three weeks, there was not a room in the mill fit to live in. Every wall had been pulled down,

71

every floor had been taken up, every ceiling had had a hole knocked in it. And then, as suddenly as they had begun, the ghost's visits ceased; and my brother-in-law was left in peace, to rebuild the place at his leisure.

'What induced the old image to play such a silly trick upon a family man and a ratepayer? Ah! That's just what I cannot tell you.'

Some said that the ghost of the wicked old man had done it to punish my brother-in-law for not believing in him at first; while others held that the apparition was probably that of some deceased local plumber and glazier, who would naturally take an interest in seeing a house knocked about and spoilt. But nobody knew anything for certain.

The Scene of the Crime

GERALD KERSH

The Big Man with the Little Black Bag turned to the right at The Bricklayers, walked on and turned right again at St George's Church. Then he found that he was lost. Someone had misdirected him, or he had misinterpreted the direction. He stood in a small curved street of cheap and pretentious houses with plaster columns, and basements fenced in with massive, spear-headed iron railings. The snow, trampled to slush in the main road, lay here like a sheepskin rug. Something like a pancake of yellow light lay under every lamp-post. The Big Man with the Little Black Bag was aware of a certain uneasiness.

Then he saw the policeman.

The policeman was standing in the penumbra beyond one of the circles of light. The top of his helmet bobbed seven feet above the snow. He was enormous in his heavy greatcoat. The Big Man with the Little Black Bag approached, with a certain trepidation, and said: 'I beg pardon, but I seem to have lost my way. Can you tell me the way to Mahogany Road?'

The policeman replied: 'Mahogany Road, sir? Yes, sir. Let me see now, Mahogany Road. This is Tulip Crescent. Follow the Crescent around to your left, just as you're going, then bear right along Jade Street, and when you get to a public-house called The Jolly Farmers, turn sharp right and there you are.'

The Big Man with the Little Black Bag said: 'Did you say Tulip Crescent? Now where have I heard Tulip Crescent mentioned before?'

The policeman said: 'I daresay you would have heard of it in connection with the Joyce Murder.'

'Oh yes, yes, the Joyce Murder, Tulip Crescent. Of course,' said the other uneasily. 'Somewhat before my time, I believe.'

'I daresay it would be,' said the policeman, 'but I remember it.'

'It happened at No. 14, I believe?'

'Yes, sir, it happened at No. 14. But after the scandal they changed the number of the house, and the number is now 13b. Yes, sir, if you want to get to Mahogany Road, follow the Crescent around to your left, then bear right along Jade Street, and when you get to a public-house called The Jolly Farmers, turn sharp right and there you are.'

The Big Man with the Little Black Bag walked on, and the policeman walked with him. From time to time, the policeman flashed his lamp into a doorway. Once he tried a lock.

'Live near here?' he asked.

The other replied: 'No, I live in Australia, in Sydney—near Sydney, at least. Not far from Sydney. I daresay you wonder what brings me here. Well, as a matter of fact, it *is* rather extraordinary but I have to go to

74

Mahogany Road to meet a distant relation of mine who I have never met before. It's a family affair. And so *this* is Tulip Crescent?'

The policeman said, with something like relish: 'This is Tulip Crescent.'

He turned and threw the beam of his light upon the door of a house.

The Big Man with the Little Black Bag saw 13b in brass against green paint in a halo of dried-up metal polish. 'It was before my time,' he said.

The policeman eased his knees and beat his gloved hands together, and said: 'It was quite a case, sir, as you may have read.'

'An old lady and an old gentleman were murdered, I believe, and no one ever found out who did it,' said the stranger.

'That's right, and after thirty years the murderer is still undiscovered,' said the policeman.

'It means that he is still at large,' said the Big Man with the Little Black Bag. 'Still at large.'

The policeman cleared his throat judicially and said: 'At least he has never been brought to court. You understand, sir, that this is my beat and I know a good deal about it. It is my business to know what goes on, and what has gone on, sir, on my beat.'

'But this was thirty years ago.'

'Yes, sir, but we have our proper professional interest in these things. I am only an ordinary police constable, as you see. But these things are interesting. And if, as I might say, I walk up and down past No. 14—or, I should say, 13b—many times every night, it is only natural for me to take an interest. You know the facts of the case, I presume?'

The Big Man with the Little Black Bag, shifting from foot to foot and looking nervously up and down the deserted Crescent, said: 'An old lady and her brother were murdered for their money, and the murderer got away scot-free, that's all I know. And now if you'll excuse me—'

The policeman, beating away the cold with his gloved hands, said: 'It was an interesting case, sir. Mr Spoon of the *Sunday Special* wrote very intelligently about it in his *Unsolved Murder Mysteries*. There was Miss Joyce and her brother, Mr Joyce. They lived in what was then No. 14, you see, sir. The Joyces were people of independent means. But I daresay you've read all about this in *Unsolved Murder Mysteries*, by the gentleman whose name I have already mentioned.'

'No, no.'

'The father was an actuary, whatever that may be, sir.'

'I believe it is a man who guesses the odds in insurance, officer.'

'I see you're a betting man, sir,' said the policeman.

'No, no, not at all,' said the Big Man with the Little Black Bag. 'I never bet.'

The policeman continued: 'Their father was an actuary, and he left the lady, Miss Joyce, a considerable sum of money. Her brother, Mr Joyce, was, if I may say so, sir, a briefless barrister, who liked his bottle and got around to living on his sister—if you get what I mean, sir.'

'Yes, yes.'

'You understand, of course, that I have studied all this pretty closely, sir, this being my beat.'

'Naturally.'

'The old lady—she was a few years older than her

brother—didn't trust banks and kept most of her money, or at least a good deal of it, in the house. A bad principle,' said the policeman. 'For my part, give me a bank.'

'Give me a bank,' said the Big Man with the Little Black Bag.

'Well, sir, the inevitable, as they say in the newspapers, is bound to happen. One dark night there was a murder,' said the policeman with gusto, 'a murder of almost unprecedented brutality. The criminal went into No. 14 as it was then, murdered the old lady, murdered the old gentleman and ran off with every farthing he could lay his hands on. It amounted to something like six hundred and twenty-five pounds six shillings and threepence.'

The other said: 'Where was the policeman on duty here, at that time?'

The policeman replied: 'This was over thirty years ago, sir, and things were a little looser in the Force then than they are at the present time. True, your police constable had to account for his movements, but there was not quite the check-up then that you get now. Your sergeants came round of course. But the policeman who was on duty here at the time of the Joyce Murder had the whole Crescent to cover and this Crescent makes a considerable bend, as you'll see by the time you get to Mahogany Road. The man who killed poor Miss Joyce and her poor brother must have watched the movements of the policeman on the beat. You know that we are usually at a certain place within a certain time. The whole thing was done in a few minutes. A few minutes? One minute, two minutes at the most. The culprit had means of entry to the house, went in, did his work, and came out, shutting the door behind him. We should not have

77

discovered the fact for days, perhaps, if the old gentleman—I mean Miss Joyce's brother—had not managed to drag himself to the front door before he died. How he managed to do it nobody knows. His skull was smashed. It was a horrible affair, as you may well imagine, and that is why they changed the number of the house. Then, of course, there was no housing shortage, and people preferred not to live in a place where such things had happened. And so, as the gentleman said in the newspaper, it remains an unsolved mystery.'

The Big Man with the Little Black Bag said: 'Were there no clues?'

The policeman replied: 'Not one. It happened about ten o'clock one night in September. If it had been wet, there might have been footprints. It was one of those dry, dusty nights, with a bit of a breeze blowing. The officer on duty observed that this crime had been committed because, in the first place, he saw that the door of No. 14 was shut. In the second place . . . '

'Did you say *shut*?' asked the Big Man with the Little Black Bag.

'Yes, sir. He was accustomed to hear from Mr and Miss Joyce at about that time. The old gentleman was not afraid of anything. He was a lawyer. But the old lady, who kept the purse-strings, she liked to be friendly with the police and, therefore, she made a point of giving the officer on duty a cake, or a pie or a sandwich—sometimes a glass of rum—late in the evening. For the first time in seven years there was silence in No. 14. The officer on duty stopped at the door of No. 14, flashing his lamp about and wondering what had happened. Then, all of a sudden, he saw a red blob creeping out under the front door. He knocked, and nobody answered, he rammed his shoulder against the door, nearly fell inside because the door was not quite caught. Then he saw poor old Mr Joyce with his head beaten in on the doormat.'

The stranger said: 'And there was an end of the matter?'

The policeman nodded. 'There was the end of the matter. Nobody found anything. There was no evidence. They questioned Miss Joyce's nephew, but he was paralysed and had been in bed for the past three years, so *he* was out of the question. It was one of those cases in which Scotland Yard was baffled, sir, baffled. The man was never caught.'

The Big Man with the Little Black Bag glanced uneasily from left to right and said: 'Do you believe that criminals—I mean murderers—feel, as they say, compelled to come back to the scene of the crime?'

'Some do, and some do not,' said the policeman.

The stranger said: 'I can understand that a man might want to come back. I can't imagine what for, but I can imagine a sort of nervous compulsion. I can simply *imagine* it, mind you . . .'

The policeman said: 'You're living in Mahogany Road?'

The stranger said: 'Which reminds me that I must be getting along. Oh, by the way, what happened to the officer on duty at that time?'

The policeman said: 'He was dismissed the Force. He used to go into the doorway of No. 102 to have a smoke. On the night of the murder it seems he had more than one smoke. He failed in his duty, sir.'

'So the criminal was never found.'

'Never found, no. But what you were saying about murderers coming back, sir. It really does happen sometimes.'

'I daresay,' said the Big Man with the Little Black Bag. 'Were there no finger-prints?'

'The murderer was wearing—'

The policeman looked down at his gloved hands.

'The policeman could have done it,' said the stranger.

'He did,' said the policeman.

Then the Big Man with the Little Black Bag found himself alone in the Crescent, and there were no footprints in the snow except his own.

In Black and White

JAN MARK

Jenny Fielding is Mrs Sanderson, now. She has a husband, two daughters, Julia and Margery, and three grandchildren. On the sideboard in the living-room stand photographs of them all; daughters, sons-in-law, granddaughters, grandson. Every year Julia and Margery send new school photographs of Angus, Alice, and Rose. Mrs Sanderson arranges them on the sideboard and puts last year's photographs in her dressing-table drawer.

On the wall, above the sideboard, hangs Mr Sanderson's school photograph. It is black and white and a metre long, the whole school in it together. One after another Angus and Alice and Rose have asked, 'Grandpa, how was it done?' and Mr Sanderson explains that once upon a time all school photographs were like that, and had to be taken with a special camera. Everybody was arranged in a huge semicircle—there were seven hundred people at his school, and the camera, which was clockwork, slowly turned, panning from one end of the

81

curve to the other. The real miracle is that, in the photograph, everyone is standing in a straight line while the building behind them looks curved. Grandpa tries to show them why, but they can never quite understand.

'You had to stand absolutely still,' Mr Sanderson says, 'because you could never be sure when the camera was pointing exactly at you.'

Angus and Alice and Rose love it when he gets to that point because they know what is coming next. Mr Sanderson is in the middle of the fourth row, looking very young and serious, with a surprising amount of hair, but at either end of the second row are the Schofeldt Triplets.

'Really, they were twins, Marcus and Ben,' Mr Sanderson tells them, 'and they were standing one each end of the row. When the camera got half-way round Ben left his place and ran along the back of the others, faster than the camera was moving, and went to stand beside Marcus at the other end. They got into a terrible row when they were found out, but we all thought they were heroes because we'd been forbidden to do it.'

Then Angus, Alice, and Rose look closely at Grandpa's school photograph to admire the three identical and heroic Schofeldt Twins, Ben at one end, Ben and Marcus at the other.

'Lots of school photographs had mysterious identical twins at each end,' Grandpa boasts, 'but I bet ours was the only one with triplets.'

'Did you have a school photograph, Granny?' Rose asks.

'I did once,' Mrs Sanderson says, vaguely, 'but I must have lost it.'

She hates lying, but if she told the truth about her school photograph no one would believe her anyway, so she pretends it is lost. But at the back of her dressing-table drawer, where Angus and Alice and Rose also lie, growing older and larger each year, is Jenny Fielding's school photograph, still rolled into a cylinder as it was on the day she first brought it home, forty years ago. She has never shown it to anyone since.

Jenny was thirteen, in the third year, when the notice was given out in assembly that the photographer was coming the following Monday. Miss Shaw, the form teacher, had a few words of her own to add when they returned to the classroom.

'You will all make sure that your uniforms are clean and pressed, that your hair is tidy—you'd better plait yours, Maureen Blake—and your shoes polished. I do not *care* if nobody can see your feet. There will be a rehearsal on Friday, so that each girl knows where she is to stand. And wherever you stand on Friday,' said Miss Shaw, fixing them with an iron gaze, 'you will stand on Monday. On these occasions there are always certain stupid people who imagine that it is amusing to run from one end of the line to the other in order to appear twice. Anyone who does that will be dealt with severely. Do I make myself clear?'

3a gazed back at her unblinkingly. Miss Shaw, as always, had made herself very clear. But in the back row Jenny's great friend Margery Fletcher turned her head slightly and muttered to Jenny, 'I bet it will be one of us. I have a feeling.'

'Did you speak, Margery?' Miss Shaw enquired, knowing perfectly well.

'I just said I thought I might get my hair cut,' Margery said, pleasantly. 'For the photograph, you know.'

'An excellent idea,' Miss Shaw said. Margery's hair,

like Jenny's, was wild and dark and curly. They were very alike in other ways, too; exactly the same height, short and stocky, and were often mistaken for each other by people who saw them misbehaving from a distance. Margery misbehaved far more frequently, and far more inventively, than Jenny, but when Jenny was falsely accused Margery always raised her hand and owned up. And on the rarer occasions when the mistake was in Jenny's favour, Jenny did the same. That was why they were best friends, faithful and true. They went everywhere together, near enough.

It had come as a surprise to no one when the announcement was made in assembly; bush telegraph had seen to that. Everybody had known for weeks that the photographer was due and some people even claimed—wrongly as it turned out—to know the date. So it was already public knowledge that after the rehearsal on Friday morning the lottery would take place. They had to wait until Friday to find out who would be in it.

Friday involved a great deal of standing about in a chilly damp wind on the lawn in front of the school. In the centre of the lawn stood a long curved row of eighty chairs, with a row of benches behind them and a row of tables behind that. One after another the classes stepped forward to take their places. On the chairs sat the sixth form with the teachers in the middle and the Headmistress in the very centre. In front of them the second years knelt upright, the most uncomfortable position of all, and right at the front sat the first years, cross-legged and trying not to show their knickers. Because they were only first years people thought that they were too young to care.

The third years stood on the grass behind the sixth form and staff, the fourth year stood behind them on the benches, and at the back the fifth forms teetered on the tables. Symmetry was all. The tallest in every group stood in the middle, the shortest at the sides, and so it was that Jenny and Margery found themselves facing each other across the grass at opposite ends of the third year, and Jenny was remembering what Margery had said last week: 'I bet it will be one of us.' There was a very good chance that it would be, one chance in four, but if it were, Jenny would be the one. Jenny was on the left, the end that the camera started from.

The entrants for the lottery met at the back of the sports pavilion after lunch; Jenny from the third year, one from the second year, one from the fourth and one from the fifth; all the left-hand tail-enders, except for the first year who were considered too young to be trusted, and the sixth who were above such things. Glenda Alcott, the fifth former, was there before them, holding her blue felt school hat in which lay four tightly folded pieces of paper.

'Now then,' Glenda said, 'three of these are blank and one carries the Black Spot. Whoever draws the Black Spot is the one who changes ends. As soon as the camera is pointing to the middle you leave your place and run round to the other end of the line. You know you'll get into a row afterwards. Are you prepared to risk it?'

The other three nodded solemnly.

'All right, then. Draw your papers.'

Madeline Enderby from the second year drew first, then Jenny, then Dawn Fuggle from the fourth, and that left one paper in the hat for Glenda and she took it out last of all.

Madeline, Dawn, and Glenda looked at each other before they looked at their papers, smiling but grim, as if they had been drawing lots to see who should go to the guillotine, but Jenny just stared at her folded paper, remembering what Margery had said: 'I bet it will be one of us. I have a feeling.' Margery had had feelings before, and they had come true. She had had a feeling before the carol concert last year, that she would be singing the descant in *Adeste Fideles*, and when Susan Beale lost her voice just before they were due to start it had been Margery who was called out to take her place. Then she had had a feeling about the geometry exam that everyone had been so worried about before Easter. 'I have a feeling there won't be an exam,' said Margery, who had done no revision, and on the morning that it was due to take place, Miss Ogden's briefcase, containing the papers, was stolen on the train.

'I have a feeling Cranmer House won't win the acting prize this year,' Margery said, the day before the drama competition, although Cranmer House were a dead cert, and sure enough, on the day, Cranmer went to pieces and fluffed their lines and missed their cues and the cup was awarded to Becket House. Margery and Jenny were in Becket.

Margery's feelings always seemed to involve misfortune for someone, Jenny sometimes reflected, but you couldn't blame Margery for that. *She* hadn't given Susan laryngitis, or nicked Miss Ogden's briefcase. Margery hadn't nobbled the entire cast of Cranmer's play.

'Open your papers,' Glenda said, and Jenny unfolded the little wad in her hand. She hardly needed to look; she knew that it would be her paper that bore the Black Spot.

'You can't back out now,' Dawn said, half envious, half relieved, when Jenny continued to stare at the paper in her palm.

'Remember what I said,' Glenda was admonishing

her. 'Wait until the camera's half-way round in case you're still in shot, then run like hell.' Madeline gasped. She was only a second year. It seemed to her a very desperate thing that grown-up Glenda should say 'hell'.

'And another thing,' Glenda said. 'Don't tell anybody else who's won, except you, Jenny. You must appoint a liaison officer. If you're going to be feeble and come down with something at the last moment you must let us know before Monday lunchtime, so that we three can draw again.'

Jenny knew that there was no chance that she would come down with anything or Margery would have mentioned it, but she had to do what Glenda said, just in case. 'Will you be my liaison officer?' Jenny asked Margery, who showed no surprise when Jenny silently handed her the Black Spot.

'No need,' Margery said. 'If anything happens to you I'll run instead.'

'But you'd have to swap ends,' Jenny said. 'It doesn't work if you run the other way. You don't show up at all.'

'That won't be hard,' Margery said. 'People will think it's you anyway. They usually do. Actually,' she added, 'I have a feeling I may have to do it.'

'Why, am I going to drop dead before Monday?' Jenny snapped. Suddenly she felt that she had had enough of Margery and her feelings.

'Only joking,' Margery said, but Jenny had turned away with an angry flounce. During country dancing that afternoon, she chose Diana Sullivan for her partner, leaving Margery to the mercies of Galumphing Gertie the Games Mistress, who always stomped in enthusiastically to help out anyone who didn't have a partner, and at the end of the afternoon she went straight home alone instead of waiting for Margery who was in a different set for maths.

On Monday morning she made herself especially tidy, as demanded, for the photograph. Rumour had it that school photographs were always taken on Mondays so that even the scruffiest girls might look half-way presentable before they went downhill during the week.

Waiting in the form room for assembly they preened and checked each other out, even though there was the whole morning and lunch to get through before it was time for the photograph, so Jenny had only just noticed that Margery was not in the room before Miss Shaw appeared at the door and beckoned her out.

'Jenny, dear,' Miss Shaw said, as they stood in the corridor, 'I wanted a word with you before I told the others—I know Margery is a very special friend of yours.'

Jenny did not have feelings, not the way Margery did, but she knew what was coming.

'Margery had an accident yesterday,' Miss Shaw said. 'She was out for a drive with some family friends and the car door wasn't properly shut. Margery was thrown out into the road when they took a bend too sharply. She's in hospital. I'm afraid she's badly hurt.'

Jenny, excused assembly, went to sit in the cloakroom and listened to the swarming sound of rubber-shod feet as class after class converged upon the hall. The Headmistress must have made an announcement— perhaps they had all said a prayer for Margery's recovery—for at break the news was all round the school. Glenda Alcott came to find Jenny.

'You needn't run if you don't want to,' Glenda said, kindly. 'We'll understand.'

'I'll be all right,' Jenny said, 'Margery wouldn't want me to back out,' but she wasn't too bothered by what Margery would have wanted. All she knew was that if she had the photograph to worry about she might not have to think of Margery herself, lying in the hospital. 'A coma,' Miss Shaw had said. 'Severe head injuries.'

While they were all lining up after lunch, to go out on to the field, Glenda sought her out again.

'Listen,' she said, 'someone told me—someone who *knows*—' she added defiantly, 'that they do it twice, just in case anyone does run.'

'Margery had a feeling they'd do that,' Jenny said.

'The first time they don't run the film. Then if you leave your place you get caught and sent back and you don't dare try it again when they go for the take,' Glenda said. 'That's how they did it at my brother's school. They did it last time we had one here, too, but I didn't realize why. I was only a first year, then.'

If it had been Glenda alone who'd said it, Jenny would probably have doubted, and panicked, and spoiled her chance by running too soon, but as they stood there, tier upon tier, as they had on Friday, she looked across that great curve to the place where Margery ought to have been standing, and did not move. And Margery and Glenda had been right.

After the camera had swept round, and while they all stood there frozen and smirking, the little photographer blew his whistle, said, 'All right, ladies, let's do it once more, to make sure,' and redirected the camera, on its tripod, towards Jenny's end of the line. He sounded his whistle again to warn them that he was ready to start and very slowly the camera began to turn a second time. Jenny thought how sinister it looked, clicking round on its plate, but the first time she had counted the seconds until it seemed to have reached the Headmistress, slap in the middle of the curve, and now, when the moment came, she took a step backwards, turned and began to run.

She hadn't thought before about what it would be like behind the curve. The backs of the fifth years, standing on their tables, reared eight feet above her, blotting out the sun; a palisade of legs, a swathe of skirts, a battlement of heads. The curve seemed endless, for she couldn't *see* the end of it, and the camera was so far ahead of her. In her mind's eye she could see that, the little black eye, inexorably turning, and she ran faster, racing her hidden adversary on the other side of the curve.

Three yards from the end of the line she slipped. The grass was damp where it had lain all day in the shade, her foot skidded from under her and, as she was off-balance already, leaning forward for the final effort, she fell flat, heavily, and lay there winded, all the air slammed out of her lungs. She thought she was going to die, but suddenly she was able to breathe again and scrambled to her feet. But it was too late to run on. As she rose upright the wall of backs relaxed, there was a surge of muted laughter and conversation. The camera had got there first, the photographer had won and the photograph was over. Glenda Alcott, who had seen her leave and had, of course, been able to see also that she had not arrived at the far end, jumped down from the table and hurried round to find out what had happened.

'Did you fall? Bad luck. Hey, don't cry,' Glenda said, when she found Jenny weeping on the grass. Madeline and Dawn, the other tail-enders, were not so charitable.

'If you couldn't do it you might have said, and one of us could have run,' Madeline grumbled.

'I tried. I did try,' Jenny wept.

'Jenny has something on her mind,' Glenda said, severely, and the other two, remembering what it must be, became all at once very serious.

Jenny's mother came up to the school at the end of the afternoon, to meet Jenny and take her home. Jenny was far too old to be taken to and from school, but her mother had something to tell her. Margery had died at just after two o'clock, while they were having the photograph taken.

Everyone at school, girls and teachers, was kind and sympathetic to Jenny—until the photographs arrived, and then the storm broke, for there was Jenny, standing on the left-hand side of the picture, and there, in all her guilt, at the far end, was Jenny again, looking a little dishevelled and blurred, as though she had moved at the wrong moment.

'It isn't me,' Jenny kept saying.

'The truth, if you please,' said first Miss Shaw and then the Headmistress. 'Are you going to tell me that you didn't leave your place?'

'Yes, I did,' Jenny said. 'I did go, I did run round, but I never got there. I fell over.'

She was, as promised, severely dealt with; barred from this and banned from that, and everyone despised her for not admitting to what she had done, when the evidence was there in black and white, for anyone to see; except for three people. Glenda Alcott, Madeline Enderby, and Dawn Fuggle had all seen her leave her place, had all been watching the far end to see her arrive, and they alone knew that she had never got there. Lesley Wilson, the girl who was standing next but one at the end of the line and who had, on the day, been at the very end, to start with, said, 'Of course you were standing next to me. I felt your arm. Only I thought at first it was Margery—I mean, it should have been Margery, shouldn't it?'

Glenda borrowed a magnifying glass and they studied that indistinct little figure at the right-hand end of the photograph. 'It *could* be you,' she said, finally. What she didn't say, and what they were all thinking, was, 'It could be Margery.'

'She said if anything happened to me she'd be there in my place,' Jenny said. 'She had a feeling.'

This is why Mrs Sanderson keeps her school photograph in a drawer instead of hanging it on the wall beside her husband's. Even now, forty years later, she can't bring herself to explain.

The Servant

ALISON PRINCE

Ginny ran down the path. Her mother shouted after her from the back door, 'When you've got a house of your own, my girl, you can make as much mess as you like. But you're not having your pocket money until you've tidied your bedroom!'

Ginny snatched her bike out of the shed, kicked the side gate open and set off down the lane. Her mother was waving her arms frantically and shouting something, but Ginny took no notice. Summer holidays were *awful*, she fumed, pedalling fast. Just because there was no school to go to, people treated you as if you were nothing at all— just a meek little figure who had to fit in with the rest of the household and not be noticed. A handy person to boss about. Run round to the shops, Ginny, dry the dishes, Ginny, tidy your room, Ginny. It was like being a *servant*.

Ginny came to the top of Bunkers Hill and let the bike freewheel down the long slope. The wind blew her hair back and made the hot morning cooler. Below her the green landscape spread out like a toy farmyard. Further down, Bunkers Hill crossed the busy main road and became Nebbutts Lane, leading through the distant fields to Cuckoo Wood where the bluebells grew so thickly in the spring. Much nearer, just before the crossroads, a disused track wandered off to the right. Ginny touched her brakes to check the bike's speed as she approached the junction. Nothing happened.

Panic clutched at Ginny's heart like a cold hand. The sunny day was whistling past her with a speed which made her eyes run. She grabbed repeatedly at the useless brakes, remembering now that she had told her father when he came home from work last night that they needed adjusting. The brakes had been slack yesterday, but now they had completely gone. And she was hurtling towards the busy highway. To go out there at this speed meant almost certain death.

There was only one escape. The track. A milk float was coming up the hill towards her, threatening to block the entry to Ginny's haven unless she got there first. She crouched over the handlebars to increase the bike's breakneck speed and banked the bike hard to her right. She missed the oncoming milk float by inches and caught a glimpse of the driver's startled face as she shot down the stony, disused lane.

The bicycle jumped and rattled over the rough surface but, to Ginny's relief, the track began to level out as it narrowed to an overgrown path between dark trees and straggling banks of brambles. Impeded by the long grass, the bike slowed down and at last stopped. Ginny got off shakily. Her knees and elbows felt as if they had turned to water.

After a few minutes she bent down and looked at the bike's brakes. They had been disconnected and the blocks removed. Her father must have been intending to buy some new ones for her today. But why hadn't he *said*? True, she had been out at a disco last night, but he could have left a note or told her mother . . . Ginny had an uneasy memory of her mother shouting something after her as she rode off this morning, but she thrust the thought away. Her parents simply didn't *care*, she told herself with a new burst of anger after being so frightened.

And now what? She had come out with every intention of staying out until lunchtime and she didn't want to go crawling home again so soon, no doubt to be bossed about and scolded for not stopping to listen to what her mother had been saying. Ginny propped the bike against the ivy-clad trunk of a tree and stared round her. It was very, very quiet. The trees seemed almost to meet overhead, shutting out the sunshine. Ginny gave a little shiver. And then she heard the bell.

It was a faint, tinkling bell, very distant. It rang with a peremptory rapidness as if shaken by an impatient hand. Somebody wanted something, and quickly. Ginny pushed her hands into her jeans pockets and set off along the path, leaving the bike where it was. Since she had nothing to do, she might as well go and find out where the sound of the bell had come from.

The path went on between its high banks in such deep shade that it was almost like being in a tunnel. Daylight glowed at its far end as if promising a clearing, and Ginny walked towards it quickly. The bell rang again, sounding closer this time. Ginny emerged from the trees to find that she had come out further along the hillside. The path ended in a field of ripening barley. Butterflies danced in the sun.

On the sloping ground beside the field, slate-roofed behind a flint wall with a gate in the middle, stood a house. Heavy lace curtains were tied in loops at its windows, and its doorstep was spotlessly white. A plume of smoke ascended from its chimney straight into the windless sky. As Ginny stared at the house, the bell sounded again, a longer, rattling tinkle. A looped curtain twitched back in the ground-floor window to the left of the front door and a face looked out. White hair, a high-necked blouse and two black eyes which stared accusingly.

'Violet! Come along in at once!' snapped a dry voice, and a finger tapped on the pane.

Ginny glanced over her shoulder in case somebody called Violet was standing behind her, but she was alone. The butterflies danced above the motionless barley.

The bell tinkled again, and this time Ginny's hand reached for the latch of the gate and she found herself running up the path. The untrodden whiteness of the front doorstep warned her not to enter this way, and she darted round the side of the house to where blue-flowered periwinkles fringed a paved yard. The back door stood open.

The large, dim kitchen had a red tiled floor, and a huge wooden plate rack stood above the stone sink like an ominous, complicated cage. Ginny found that she was listening intently, in a kind of dread. She was waiting for the bell to ring. In a few moments its jangling tinkle sounded, so close that it was almost inside her head. She ran through the shadowed hall, where patches of red and blue light gleamed from a panel of stained glass in the front door, and tapped on the white-painted door to her right.

'Come *in*,' said the dry voice impatiently.

Ginny opened the sitting-room door. The fingers which gripped the small brass bell by its ebony handle were thin and bony, the hand blue-veined, veiled by a ruffle of lace from the tight silk sleeve. Tiny jet buttons ran up the narrow bodice to the cameo at the high neck, and then there was the white face, the mouth thin and pinched and the nose as craggy as a parrot's beak, the eyes astonishingly black under the elaborate pile of white hair.

'You are not to go outside, Violet,' said the woman. 'You belong in here, with me.'

Ginny found that she was standing with her hands behind her and her feet together, and almost smiled at her own sudden politeness. 'My name's Ginny,' she said.

'Not suitable,' said the woman heavily. The black eyes travelled slowly down Ginny's figure until they reached her plimsolls, then travelled up again. Vertical lines appeared above the lips as the mouth tightened a little more.

'Violet,' said the woman, 'you will wear your uniform at all times in this house, do you understand?'

'But I'm not—' began Ginny. Her voice petered out as the tight lips smiled grimly.

'Oh, yes, you are, my dear,' said the woman. 'My servants have always been called Violet. So much more convenient. I am Mrs Rackham, but you will call me madam, of course.'

Ginny shook her head in confusion. This could not be happening. But she looked at the little brass bell with the ebony handle, and stared into Mrs Rackham's black, unblinking eyes, and knew that it was true.

'I have been *waiting* for my breakfast,' said Mrs Rackham.

Ginny stared guiltily into the black eyes, struggling to hold on to the idea that Mrs Rackham's breakfast had nothing to do with her, Ginny Thompson.

Mrs Rackham leaned forward a little. 'Light the spirit lamp,' she instructed impatiently, 'then go to the kitchen and get my breakfast.' The blue-veined hand gestured towards the table which stood by the window, draped with a lace cloth over heavy red chenille. On it stood eggshell-thin cups and saucers, a silver teapot and sugar bowl and a thin-spouted brass kettle which, supported on a brass stand, stood over a small burner. Ginny moved towards it. At any rate, she thought, it was better than hanging about at home. If she was treated like a servant there, she might just as well play at being a servant here.

A box of matches lay beside the brass kettle. Ginny struck one and turned up the wick in its holder. It burned with a steady blue flame. The old woman was mad, of course, Ginny told herself. It wasn't unusual in old people. Her own granny had been very absent-minded, always calling Ginny by the name of a long-dead aunt, Flora, which was even worse than Violet.

'That's better,' said Mrs Rackham, darting a black-eyed glance at the spirit lamp. 'Now get along to the kitchen, quickly. When you bring my breakfast, you will be properly dressed.'

Ginny smiled and said, 'All right.'

Mrs Rackham looked outraged. 'That is not the way to answer,' she snapped. 'Say, "yes, madam." And curtsy.'

Ginny held out imaginary skirts and curtsied deeply as she had been taught at her ballet class.

Mrs Rackham seemed even more angry. 'Just a small bob, you stupid creature!' she hissed. 'Do you girls know *nothing* these days?'

Ginny expected to feel amused as she gave an obedient little bob, but as Mrs Rackham growled, 'That's better,' and the black eyes bored into Ginny's mind, the hidden smile shrivelled and died.

Ginny left the room with quick, neat footsteps, closing the door quietly behind her. As she made her way back to the kitchen the voice of reason in her mind urged her to walk out of the door and back along the lane to her brakeless bicycle, and start pushing it home. On the other hand . . . Mrs Rackham had to have her breakfast. Perhaps whoever looked after her had gone out for a while. No doubt they would be back.

The kitchen was cool and quiet. Greenish light filtered through a small, ivy-covered window, and a few flies circled aimlessly under the high ceiling. Gazing up at them, Ginny saw that a black dress and several white aprons hung from a wooden airer, and a starched white cap dangled from the end of one of its bars. She unhitched the airer's rope from its hook on the wall and released it hand over hand, lowering the airer so that she could reach the clothes. If she was going to humour the old lady's delusions, she might as well do the job properly.

But as Ginny peeled off her T-shirt and jeans she found that she was listening in a kind of terror for Mrs Rackham's bell; as if its demanding tinkle had dominated her whole life. She struggled into the black dress and did up the rows of buttons down the front and on each sleeve. She pulled on the thick black stockings which she also found on the airer, sliding up the pair of elastic garters which were looped round the airer's end beside the cap.

Then she tied on a white, lace-edged apron and pulled the starched cap over her curly hair. She looked round for something more suitable than her plimsolls and found, neatly placed beside the wooden mangle, a pair of highly-polished black shoes, fastened by a single button.

The shoes fitted as if Ginny had always worn them. She pulled up the airer, then stared round the kitchen with increasing anxiety. What did madam have for breakfast? Plates of all sizes stood in the cage-like wooden plate rack, but there seemed to be no fridge and the pantry contained no muesli or cornflakes.

Mrs Rackham's bell rang.

Ginny jumped round, a hand to the high-buttoned neck of her dress. The voice of reason seemed to have deserted her, and she could only think that madam was waiting for her breakfast and that she, Violet, had failed to get it yet. She ran to the front room.

'Do I have to wait all day?' demanded Mrs Rackham. A vigorous spurt of steam was hissing from the brass kettle over its burner.

'I—I'm sorry, madam,' stammered Ginny. 'I didn't know what you wanted.'

'Two lightly boiled eggs, brown bread and butter cut in fingers, toast and marmalade,' said Mrs Rackham. 'Stupid girl. You can make the tea now you are here.'

Ginny went across to the table. She found an ornate tea caddy and put two spoonfuls of tea into the silver teapot. Then she picked up the brass kettle—and let it fall back into its stand with a gasp of pain. The handle was almost red hot. Tears sprang to Ginny's eyes as she nursed her stinging pain, but Mrs Rackham threw herself back in her chair, convulsed with cruel laughter. 'They all burn their hands!' she cackled delightedly. 'It's always the same—again and again!' Then, just as suddenly, she was angry. 'Turn the burner down, you idiot,' she snapped. 'The room is full of steam. And fetch a kettle holder.'

In the pale light of the kitchen, Ginny looked at her hand and saw the long red weal across the palm, and wanted to sit down and cry. But Mrs Rackham's bell was ringing, and she snatched the kettle holder from its hook beside the great black range and ran back to the sitting-room. She made the tea and said, 'I'll go and boil the eggs.'

'*When* you have moved the table within my reach,' said Mrs Rackham. 'And where is the milk?'

Ginny pushed the heavy table across to the old lady's chair, hampered by the stinging pain in her hand. Then she ran back to the kitchen for the milk, which she found by some kind of instinct in a small lidded churn on the pantry shelf. She snatched a blue jug from its hook and ladled some milk into it. The bell was ringing.

'That is a *kitchen* jug!' screamed Mrs Rackham as Ginny proffered the milk, and lace ruffles flew as a hand flashed out, sweeping the jug from Ginny's hand to smash against the sideboard. 'Clear all that mess up,' Mrs Rackham commanded, her face tight with fury, 'then bring my milk in the proper jug. Where are my eggs? Don't you dare boil them for more than three minutes!'

Ginny ran sobbing to the kitchen, found a small glass jug and filled it with milk then carried it back to Mrs Rackham, who said nothing. Milk dripped from the polished edge of the mahogany sideboard.

As Ginny went in search of a cloth she tried to recall the reasonable voice which told her that she did not belong here; but there was nothing in her mind except worry and guilt and the stinging of her burned hand. She found a rather smelly piece of rag and cleaned up the spilt milk as best she could, and picked up the pieces of the broken jug.

'Violet, *where* are my eggs?' enquired Mrs Rackham.

'Coming,' said Ginny desperately.

'Coming, *madam*!' shouted Mrs Rackham.

'Coming, madam,' Ginny repeated, and went out with a little curtsy, wiping her eyes on her sleeve. The bell tinkled and she turned back.

The black eyes were fixed upon her with a new energy as the tea was sipped, the cup returned with neat precision to its saucer. 'Have you done the fires?' asked Mrs Rackham. 'Black-leaded the grates, washed the hearths, swept the carpets, dusted? Cleaned the knives, whitened the doorstep, done the washing, scrubbed the kitchen floor? And what about the bedrooms? Are the beds clean and aired?'

'I don't know,' said Ginny helplessly. Tears overwhelmed her.

'I don't know, *madam*!' screamed Mrs Rackham.

Ginny fled to the safety of the kitchen, shaking. She found eggs in a large bowl, and an egg timer with red sand in the lower half of its double-bulged shape. She took a saucepan from the shelf, still crying a little, and filled it with hot water from the huge black kettle which steamed on the range.

Ginny found that her burned hand was beginning to blister. Like a remembered dream, a voice in her head told her that she did not have to stay here. There was a memory, too, of wearing different clothes. Trousers, a shirt made of soft stuff which left her arms bare . . . Ginny wiped her eyes on her black sleeve again, with a gesture so familiar that it seemed as if she had done it many times before. She gazed round the kitchen as if seeking those other garments, but the wooden chairs with a pattern of pierced holes in the seats were bare in the dim light, and the flies circled endlessly against the high ceiling.

The water in the saucepan began to bubble, and Ginny lowered in two eggs with a spoon, then turned over the egg timer. As the trickle of red sand began to run through the narrow neck, she got a brown loaf out of the earthenware bread crock and cut two slices, biting her lip because of the pain in her hand. Then she buttered the slices and cut them neatly into fingers.

When the eggs were done, she assembled a tray and carried it through the hall to Mrs Rackham. The sitting-room was dazzling after the dim kitchen, for sunlight poured in through the long window. Outside, the barley shimmered in the sun and the butterflies danced. Tears suddenly brimmed again in Ginny's eyes. She would never be free to walk through the fields, to come so fast down a steep hill that her eyes ran, but not with tears.

'Don't stand there gawking, Violet,' said Mrs Rackham. 'Put the things down here.'

Ginny obediently slid the tray on to the lace cloth.

'Where is my toast?' demanded Mrs Rackham.

'I—I didn't know how to make it,' Ginny faltered. Remotely, she remembered making toast by putting slices of bread into little slits in the top of—of what? She shook her head, confused. She had always been here. She would never leave. She would die here.

'With a toasting fork, you stupid girl, in front of the range,' said Mrs Rackham. She decapitated an egg then added, 'The spirit lamp has gone out. Light it.'

Ginny held a burning match to the wick, but no flame sprang up.

'Refill it,' snapped Mrs Rackham, waving an irritable hand towards the corner cupboard.

Ginny opened the tall, panelled door and took out the bottle of spirit. Violet, she thought as she gazed at its wonderful purple colour. Violet. Like me.

With the kettle holder she gingerly removed the top of the burner and filled up its reservoir with spirit. Her burned hand made her clumsy and the spirit spilled over and ran down on to the lace cloth, soaking through into the red chenille below it. Ginny shot a fearful glance at Mrs Rackham, but madam was probing an egg with the delicate silver spoon, and did not look up. Ginny fed the wick carefully back into the reservoir and fitted the top into place again. Once more she struck a match and applied it to the wick.

A blue flame leapt up, not only from the wick but from the whole top of the burner, following the spilt spirit down the brass stand and on the soaked cloth under it. Ginny shrieked with terror and jumped back, brushing against the uncorked bottle of spirit with her sleeve as she did so and knocking it over. More spirit gushed out, and sheets of flame sprang up, engulfing the kettle and its stand, the teapot, the cups, the table. Mrs Rackham began to scream, her mouth wide open in the white face, her blue-veined hands upraised. The red chenille cloth was ablaze, and the varnish on the heavy mahogany table legs was wrinkling as it caught fire. Flames began to leap up the side of the chintz arm chair where Mrs Rackham sat, still screaming. The skirt of her silk dress shrivelled as the flames licked across the chair, and Ginny saw that Mrs Rackham's legs were as twisted and useless as a rag doll's, encased in heavy contraptions of iron and leather.

Outside, the dancing butterflies shivered behind a screen of heat as the looped curtains burned. The room filled with smoke, and Ginny began to gasp for breath. Suddenly she realized that she must get out. She could not help Mrs Rackham. The hem of her long black dress was beginning to smoulder as she ran from the room. She grappled with the bolt on the front door. Her dress was burning. The house was full of fire, and the red and blue stained glass windows in the front door were dimmed with the choking smoke.

As Ginny wrenched the door open and daylight burst upon her like an explosion it seemed that Mrs Rackham was screaming a single word, senselessly and repeatedly.

'Again!' she shrieked, and it was like a mad song of agony and triumph. 'Again! Again! Again!' And Ginny knew what the terrible word meant. Like a recurring nightmare whose end only leads to the next beginning, she was condemned to repeat this experience over and over again. Even now, as the air fanned her burning dress into greedy flames and the screams were swallowed up in the inferno which had been a house; even in the agony of burning alive, Ginny was listening for the tinkle of Mrs Rackham's bell. It would all begin again.

Somebody was shaking her. 'Ginny!' a voice was saying urgently. 'Are you all right? What are you doing here?'

Mrs Thompson stared down at her daughter, who lay huddled by the rusted gate in the flint wall, an arm flung protectively across her face. She appeared to be asleep.

'Again,' said Ginny, and trembled.

'Are you all right?' Mrs Thompson repeated. 'I was frantic when you went off like that—your dad said to tell you about the bike, that he'd get new brake blocks. He'll murder me. Then the milkman said you nearly crashed into him tearing down Bunkers Hill—well, I got the car out straight away and came down here looking for you.'

Ginny's eyes were open but she was not seeing her mother. Her gaze searched the sky with a kind of despair. 'Butterflies,' she murmured. Tears welled up and she rubbed her eyes on the back of her wrist wearily.

'Darling, don't cry,' said her mother. 'It's all right— I'm not cross or anything. I mean, it was partly my fault.' After a pause she went on, 'I found your bike along the lane. But why did you come here? I hate ruined houses, they're so creepy.' Rose bay willow herb, the fire weed, stood tall among the blackened heaps of stone. It really was a horrible place, Mrs Thompson thought. Some distance away the remains of a brass kettle lay dented and squashed in the sun.

Ginny stood up and brushed fussily at her bare arms, fiddling at her wrists as though buttoning tight cuffs. Her mother watched with dawning concern as the girl straightened an apron, smoothed out a long skirt, her anxious hands not touching the surface of her jeans. 'I must go,' she said.

'You're not going anywhere,' said Ginny's mother. 'You're coming home with me. You must have had a nasty shock. We can put your bike in the back of the car.'

Ginny gave a sudden start. 'I must go,' she said again with worried alertness. 'Mrs Rackham wants her breakfast. That's her bell. What am I doing out here?'

Her mother stared. 'Mrs Rackham? This house is known as Rackham's, yes, but there's nobody here now. Some old crippled woman owned it, they say, but she died in the fire when it was burnt down, along with some poor little servant girl.'

'Violet,' agreed Ginny. She dropped a small curtsy, not looking at her mother, and called, 'Coming, madam!' Then she set off with oddly neat little footsteps through the weed-grown rubble, trotting parallel to the garden wall until she turned at a right angle and ran on to where some blue-flowered periwinkle bloomed among the stone. Her mother intercepted her and caught the girl by the hand. Ginny flinched violently. A long, red, blistered weal lay across her palm.

'How on earth did you do that?' demanded her mother. 'There's nothing hot on a bicycle. Unless—you didn't put your hand on the tyre, did you, to try to stop?'

But Ginny did not hear. She was staring into the black eyes again, watching the thin mouth in the white face as the orders were snapped out, hearing the cruel laughter as she burned her hand again. Outside the tall window, the barley shimmered in the summer sun and the butterflies danced. But Ginny would never be free to walk among them again. She was Mrs Rackham's servant and madam wanted her breakfast. Again—and again—and again.

A Pair of Muddy Shoes

LENNOX ROBINSON

I am going to try to write it down quite simply, just as it happened. I shall try not to exaggerate anything.

I am twenty-two years old, my parents are dead, I have no brothers or sisters; the only near relation I have is Aunt Margaret, my father's sister. She is unmarried and lives alone in a little house in the country in the west of county Cork. She is kind to me and I often spend my holidays with her, for I am poor and have few friends.

I am a school-teacher—that is to say, I teach drawing and singing. I am a visiting teacher at two or three schools in Dublin. I make a fair income, enough for a single woman to live comfortably on, but father left debts behind him, and until these are paid off I have to live very simply. I suppose I ought to eat more and eat better food. People sometimes think I am nervous and highly strung: I look rather fragile and delicate, but really I am not. I have slender hands, with pale, tapering fingers—the sort of hands people call 'artistic'.

I hoped very much that my aunt would invite me to spend Christmas with her. I happened to have very little money; I had paid off a big debt of poor father's, and that left me very short, and I felt rather weak and ill. I didn't quite know how I'd get through the holidays unless I went down to my aunt's. However, ten days before Christmas the invitation came. You may be sure I accepted it gratefully, and when my last school broke up on the 20th I packed my trunk, gathered up the old sentimental songs Aunt Margaret likes best, and set off for Rosspatrick.

It rains a great deal in West Cork in the winter: it was raining when Aunt Margaret met me at the station. 'It's been a terrible month, Peggy,' she said, as she turned the pony's head into the long road that runs for four muddy miles from the station to Rosspatrick. 'I think it's rained every day for the last six weeks. And the storms! We lost a chimney two days ago: it came through the roof, and let the rain into the ceiling of the spare bedroom. I've had to make you up a bed in the lumber-room till Jeremiah Driscoll can be got to mend the roof.'

I assured her that any place would do me; all I wanted was her society and a quiet time.

'I can guarantee you those,' she said. 'Indeed, you look tired out: you look as if you were just after a bad illness or just before one. That teaching is killing you.'

That lumber-room was really very comfortable. It was a large room with two big windows; it was on the ground floor, and Aunt Margaret had never used it as a bedroom because people are often afraid of sleeping on the ground floor.

We stayed up very late talking over the fire. Aunt Margaret came with me to my bedroom; she stayed there for a long time, fussing about the room, hoping I'd be comfortable, pulling about the furniture, looking at the bedclothes.

At last I began to laugh at her. 'Why shouldn't I be comfortable? Think of my horrid little bedroom in Brunswick Street! What's wrong with this room?'

'Nothing—oh, nothing,' she said rather hurriedly, and kissed me and left me.

I slept very well. I never opened my eyes till the maid called me, and then after she had left me I dozed off again. I had a ridiculous dream. I dreamed I was interviewing a rich old lady: she offered me a thousand a year and comfortable rooms to live in. My only duty was to keep her clothes from moths; she had quantities of beautiful, costly clothes, and she seemed to have a terror of them being eaten by moths. I accepted her offer at once. I remember saying to her gaily, 'The work will be no trouble to me, I like killing moths.'

It was strange I should say that, because I really don't like killing moths—I hate killing anything. But my dream was easily explained, for when I woke a second later (as it seemed), I was holding a dead moth between my finger and thumb. It disgusted me just a little bit—that dead moth pressed between my fingers, but I dropped it quickly, jumped up, and dressed myself.

Aunt Margaret was in the dining-room, and full of profuse and anxious enquiries about the night I had spent. I soon relieved her anxieties, and we laughed together over my dream and the new position I was going to fill. It was very wet all day and I didn't stir out of the house. I sang a great many songs, I began a pencil-drawing of my aunt—a thing I had been meaning to make for years—but I didn't feel well, I felt headachy and nervous—just from being in the house all day, I suppose. I felt the greatest disinclination to go to bed. I felt afraid, I don't know of what.

Of course I didn't say a word of this to Aunt Margaret.

That night the moment I fell asleep I began to dream. I thought I was looking down at myself from a great height. I saw myself in my nightdress crouching in a corner of the bedroom. I remember wondering why I was crouching there, and I came nearer and looked at myself again, and then I saw that it was not myself that crouched there—it was a large white cat, it was watching a mouse-hole. I was relieved and I turned away. As I did so I heard the cat spring. I started round. It had a mouse between its paws, and looked up at me, growling as a cat does. Its face was like a woman's face—was like my face. Probably that doesn't sound at all horrible to you, but it happens that I have a deadly fear of mice. The idea of holding one between my hands, of putting my mouth to one, of—oh, I can't bear even to write it.

I think I woke screaming. I know when I came to myself I had jumped out of bed and was standing on the floor. I lit the candle and searched the room. In one corner were some boxes and trunks; there might have been a mouse-hole behind them, but I hadn't the courage to pull them out and look. I kept my candle lighted and stayed awake all night.

The next day was fine and frosty. I went for a long walk in the morning and for another in the afternoon. When bedtime came I was very tired and sleepy. I went to sleep at once and slept dreamlessly all night.

It was the next day that I noticed my hands getting queer. 'Queer' perhaps isn't the right word, for, of course, cold does roughen and coarsen the skin, and the weather was frosty enough to account for that. But it wasn't only that the skin was rough, the whole hand looked larger, stronger, not like my own hand. How ridiculous this sounds, but the whole story is ridiculous.

I remember once, when I was a child at school, putting on another girl's boots by mistake one day. I had to go about till evening in them, and I was perfectly miserable. I could not stop myself from looking at my feet, and they seemed to me to be the feet of another person. That sickened me, I don't know why. I felt a little like that now when I looked at my hands. Aunt Margaret noticed how rough and swollen they were, and she gave me cold cream which I rubbed on them before I went to bed.

I lay awake for a long time. I was thinking of my hands. I didn't seem to be able not to think of them. They seemed to grow bigger and bigger in the darkness; they seemed monstrous hands, the hands of some horrible ape, they seemed to fill the whole room. Of course if I had struck a match and lit the candle I'd have calmed myself in a minute, but, frankly, I hadn't the courage. When I touched one hand with the other it seemed rough and hairy, like a man's.

At last I fell asleep. I dreamed that I got out of bed and opened the window. For several minutes I stood looking out. It was bright moonlight and bitterly cold. I felt a great desire to go for a walk. I dreamed that I dressed myself quickly, put on my slippers, and stepped out of the window. The frosty grass crunched under my feet. I walked, it seemed for miles, along a road I never remember being on before. It led uphill; I met no one as I walked.

Presently I reached the crest of the hill, and beside the road, in the middle of a bare field, stood a large house. It was a gaunt three-storeyed building, there was an air of decay about it. Maybe it had once been a gentleman's place, and was now occupied by a herd. There are many places like that in Ireland. In a window of the highest storey there was a light. I decided I would go to the house and ask the way home. A gate closed the grass-grown avenue from the road; it was fastened and I could not open it, so I climbed it. It was a high gate but I climbed it easily, and I remember thinking in my dream, 'If this wasn't a dream I could never climb it so easily.'

I knocked at the door, and after I had knocked again the window of the room in which the light shone was opened, and a voice said, 'Who's there? What do you want?'

It came from a middle-aged woman with a pale face and dirty strands of grey hair hanging about her shoulders.

I said, 'Come down and speak to me; I want to know the way back to Rosspatrick.'

I had to speak two or three times to her, but at last she came down and opened the door mistrustfully. She only opened it a few inches and barred my way. I asked her the road home, and she gave me directions in a nervous, startled way.

Then I dreamed that I said, 'Let me in to warm myself.'

'It's late; you should be going home.'

But I laughed, and suddenly pushed at the door with my foot and slipped past her.

I remember she said, 'My God,' in a helpless, terrified way. It was strange that she should be frightened, and I, a young girl all alone in a strange house with a strange woman, miles from anyone I knew, should not be frightened at all. As I sat warming myself by the fire while she boiled the kettle (for I had asked for tea), and watching her timid, terrified movements, the queerness of the position struck me, and I said, laughing, 'You seem afraid of me.'

'Not at all, miss,' she replied, in a voice which almost trembled.

'You needn't be, there's not the least occasion for it,' I said, and I laid my hand on her arm.

She looked down at it as it lay there, and said again, 'Oh, my God,' and staggered back against the range.

And so for half a minute we remained. Her eyes were fixed on my hand which lay on my lap; it seemed she could never take them off it.

'What is it?' I said.

'You've the face of a girl,' she whispered, 'and—God help me—the hands of a man.'

I looked down at my hands. They were large, strong and sinewy, covered with coarse red hairs. Strange to say they no longer disgusted me: I was proud of them—proud of their strength, the power that lay in them.

'Why should they make you afraid?' I asked. 'They are fine hands. Strong hands.'

But she only went on staring at them in a hopeless, frozen way.

'Have you ever seen such strong hands before?' I smiled at her.

'They're—they're Ned's hands,' she said at last, speaking in a whisper.

She put her own hand to her throat as if she were choking, and the fastening of her blouse gave way. It fell open. She had a long throat; it was moving as if she were finding it difficult to swallow. I wondered whether my hands would go round it.

Suddenly I knew they would, and I knew why my hands were large and sinewy, I knew why power had been given to them. I got up and caught her by the throat. She struggled so feebly; slipped down, striking her head against the range; slipped down on to the red-tiled floor and lay quite still, but her throat still moved under my hand and I never loosened my grasp.

And presently, kneeling over her, I lifted her head and bumped it gently against the flags of the floor. I did this again and again; lifting it higher, and striking it harder and harder, until it was crushed in like an egg, and she lay still. She was choked and dead.

And I left her lying there and ran from the house, and as I stepped on to the road I felt rain in my face. The thaw had come.

When I woke it was morning. Little by little my dream came back and filled me with horror. I looked at my hands. They were so tender and pale and feeble. I lifted them to my mouth and kissed them.

But when Mary called me half an hour later she broke into a long, excited story of a woman who had been murdered the night before, how the postman had found the door open and the dead body. 'And sure, miss, it was here she used to live long ago; she was near murdered once, by her husband, in this very room; he tried to choke her, she was half killed—that's why the mistress made it a lumber-room. They put him in the asylum afterwards; a month ago he died there I heard.'

My mother was Scottish, and claimed she had the gift of prevision. It was evident she had bequeathed it to me. I was enormously excited. I sat up in bed and told Mary my dream.

She was not very interested, people seldom are in other

people's dreams. Besides, she wanted, I suppose, to tell her news to Aunt Margaret. She hurried away. I lay in bed and thought it all over. I almost laughed, it was so strange and fantastic.

But when I got out of bed I stumbled over something. It was a little muddy shoe. At first I hardly recognized it, then I saw it was one of a pair of evening shoes I had, the other shoe lay near it. They were a pretty little pair of dark blue satin shoes, they were a present to me from a girl I loved very much, she had given them to me only a week ago.

Last night they had been so fresh and new and smart. Now they were scratched, the satin cut, and they were covered with mud. Someone had walked miles in them.

And I remembered in my dream how I had searched for my shoes and put them on.

Sitting on the bed, feeling suddenly sick and dizzy, holding the muddy shoes in my hand, I had in a blinding instant a vision of a red-haired man who lay in this room night after night for years, hating a sleeping white-faced woman who lay beside him, longing for strength and courage to choke her. I saw him come back, years afterwards—freed by death—to this room; saw him seize on a feeble girl too weak to resist him; saw him try her, strengthen her hands, and at last—through her—accomplish his unfinished deed . . . The vision passed all in a flash as it had come. I pulled myself together. 'That is nonsense, impossible,' I told myself. 'The murderer will be found before evening.'

But in my hand I still held the muddy shoes. I seem to be holding them ever since.

An Apple for Miss Stevenson

MICHAEL VESTEY

They knew January was a bad month to go house-hunting but they had no alternative. They had already sold their own house. Kent looked more like the backyard than the garden of England. Still, the Sheldons reasoned, it was the same bleak landscape in all the Home Counties and it wouldn't put them off living in the country.

Phillip Sheldon and his wife Elizabeth were both Londoners but they had made their decision to move out, like so many young couples before them. They now felt strangers in the city, and they disliked the noise, the discomfort, the poor schooling, and the growing shabbiness. Besides, there were the children to think of, or, rather, their one child, a little girl of five called Emma. Far better for her to grow up in the country than the town.

That is how they came to be standing at the lichen-cloaked gate to Rose Cottage on the edge of a village in the heart of the Kentish hop fields. Phillip shivered in the coldness of the New Year. The sky was the colour of the wood-smoke that spurted from chimney pots in the village. The trees in the rambling garden were bent like arthritics in the sharp wind. Gamekeeper's weather, thought Phillip. He wondered if he would miss their warm, centrally heated, purpose-built townhouse in the suburbs.

Elizabeth looked up at her husband and smiled. 'Well, it's big,' she said.

Phillip frowned. 'Yes . . . are you sure we've got the right place?' There was no For Sale sign evident. 'It seems too big for a cottage.'

Without knowing what the inside was like, Phillip felt instinctively that the house was a bargain. He looked down at the estate agent's particulars on a sheet of white paper flapping in his cold hands.

Elizabeth said: 'I'm amazed it hasn't gone before now. It must be awful inside.'

'Right, let's go in and see the dreadful truth,' he said, opening the gate and walking up the drive. Elizabeth was about to follow him when she felt her arm jerked backwards. It was Emma. The little girl stood firmly the other side of the gate. Her pale face could just be seen peeping through the hood of her black duffle coat and the thickly entwined scarf.

'No,' cried Emma. 'No.'

Phillip was half-way up the drive, unaware of his daughter's reluctance to follow him, when he suddenly realized he was alone. He turned, a tall, thin, pin-striped figure, wisps of dark hair blowing across his spectacles. 'Well, come on, then,' he yelled, stamping his feet. 'It's chilly out here.'

'It's Emma,' his wife replied. 'She won't come.'

'Oh God! What a time to throw a tantrum,' muttered Phillip. She'd been so good on the journey down and even at the previous house they had viewed. He could see that Emma clearly did not want to budge. What he could see of her tiny white face was set hard with determination, an expression both he and Elizabeth had learned to identify. The last time she had behaved in this way was on her first day at school.

Elizabeth crouched and put her face close to Emma's. 'Darling, we won't be long, this is the last house we'll see today. And then we can all go and have tea somewhere. Won't that be nice?'

Emma's chin trembled and her face began to crumple. She started to cry.

Phillip became impatient. 'Can't she play in the garden while we're inside?' he shouted.

'No,' replied Elizabeth. 'If she's going to live here, then she must see it first.'

'Oh well, I'm going on. You join me later.' Phillip strode up towards the house which sat on a small hill at the highest point of the garden. Weeds sprouted through the worn gravel and scattered shingle of the neglected drive. 'The garden was once a feature of the house,' he said to himself, repeating the words in the brochure. 'Not any more it isn't.' He glanced at the thick bushes, matted together like uncombed animal fur, the deep-pile lawn which would take several mowings to recover its health, and the brambles snaking across what had once clearly been a vegetable patch. The summer would be an energetic time!

A few yards from the house he stood with hands on hips and looked it over. It was timber-framed and clad in white-painted weatherboarding, some of which was peeling. The window and door frames were painted black to provide a sharp contrast. Unpruned climbing plants covered the downstairs windows, making it impossible to see inside. There were solid brick chimneys at both ends of the house, between which the sand-coloured tiled roof gently undulated.

He turned the key in the lock and with some difficulty pushed open the front door. Inside it felt damp and almost colder than it was outside. He could smell the decay caused by the moisture in the floorboards and plaster. It came as no surprise to him. After all, the agent had made it clear the house had been empty for two years.

After passing through a small lobby he found himself in what appeared to be the main sitting-room. It had wide, oak floorboards in reasonably good condition, and a huge inglenook fireplace, high enough for a man his height, six feet, to stand up in without bumping his head.

'Isn't it lovely?' said a voice behind him. Elizabeth stood in the doorway holding Emma by the arm. Neither parent noticed that Emma's face had turned a sickly grey.

'I don't know what's the matter with her. I had to promise all sorts of bribes to get her up here. There, Emma!' she said, tugging at the little girl's arm. 'What do you think?'

Emma stared with deep curiosity in the direction of the inglenook fireplace. She said nothing. Her parents shrugged, and moved towards the kitchen, which turned out to be a high-ceilinged room with black-painted oak beams running from end to end. One side of the ceiling sloped downwards to follow the line of the cat's slide roof at the rear of the house.

Upstairs there were five bedrooms, including a small

room in the roof. Elizabeth was attracted by the character of the house with its oak floors and beams; Phillip by the size of the rooms and the feeling of space in a house three hundred years old. An additional bonus was that he had bumped his head only once—on a low door frame.

'Yes,' Elizabeth murmured. 'We must have this.'

'Subject to survey and contract,' said Phillip, who, as a solicitor, was not going to allow sentiment to overwhelm him entirely. They both laughed. 'Come on, then,' said Phillip. 'Let's go back and make an offer.'

When they reached the front door they realized that Emma was not with them any more. They called out and listened. Not a sound, apart from the wind. Phillip became aware of how quiet it would be living there and he wondered, fleetingly, if he would be able to cope after the city.

'I'll go and find her,' said Elizabeth, moving towards the room with the inglenook. There she spotted Emma seated in the gloom of the fireplace engrossed in something, she couldn't see what.

'Oh, there you are, darling. Come on, we're off.'

Emma seemed startled. She glanced up at her mother, and in the poor light Elizabeth noticed a familiar expression of guilt on Emma's face. However, Elizabeth was anxious to return to the estate agent's. She held out a hand. Emma nodded, smiled and then skipped towards the front door. Surprised but also pleased at the sudden change of attitude in her daughter, Elizabeth said: 'That's better.'

At the estate agent's, the senior partner Mr Wilcox showed little enthusiasm when the Sheldons told him they wanted to buy Rose Cottage. 'You *liked* it then?' he asked cautiously, seated behind his leather-topped desk.

Phillip nodded. 'It's got more than enough for a growing family, and bags of character, of course.'

'Yes, it's certainly roomy,' replied Mr Wilcox, unscrewing the top of his fountain pen. 'It was once a school, you know.'

'A school!' both exclaimed in unison. 'It's not that big, surely?' questioned Phillip.

'No, but it was big enough to be a small prep school. It was called St Anne's.' He smiled. 'Occasionally, the local vet and the supermarket manager stop and stare over the garden gate with nostalgic looks on their faces.'

Elizabeth and Phillip gave Mr Wilcox their full attention as he gave them a brief history of the house. It was a farmhouse until the turn of the century when it was bought by a wealthy widow who lived there until the outbreak of the Second World War. She sold it to two middle-aged sisters, Amy and Charlotte Stevenson, both spinsters who ran a prep school in Dover.

Rather than risk the bombs, the sisters searched inland for suitable premises to house their school. That's how they found Rose Cottage, explained Mr Wilcox, though it wasn't called that then. Because of its size the school could cater only for about twenty-five to thirty pupils with a few boarders. In their spare time the sisters, both amateur horticulturists, transformed the garden from an ordinary patch of lawn and shrubbery into what Mr Wilcox fondly recalled as a 'scented paradise' of rare flowers and plants. 'It was lovely then,' he sighed.

'Pretty red roses,' said Emma suddenly.

Mr Wilcox glanced across at Emma who was sitting on a chair by the window. He seemed surprised. 'Yes, that's right, young lady. Miss Amy Stevenson's roses were famous in this area, especially the red ones.'

'I didn't see any roses,' said Phillip. Elizabeth shook her head.

Mr Wilcox laughed. 'All roses are red to children,' he said with a chuckle. But when he had spoken the cheerfulness gave way to a frown.

'By the way,' said Elizabeth. 'What happened to the old ladies?'

'Ah, yes.' Mr Wilcox clasped his hands together on the desktop, pursed his lips and squinted slightly through his spectacles. 'Well, they both passed on. Rather sad really: St Anne's became too much for them. In the last years they could manage only elocution lessons. That's when the school ceased and they called it Rose Cottage instead. First Miss Charlotte went, in hospital, and then Miss Amy, about a year later, I think. The house has been empty since then, as you could see from its neglect.'

'I'm surprised you haven't been able to sell it before now; it's not in that bad condition,' said Phillip.

Mr Wilcox agreed. After an initial hesitation he gave a short nervous laugh. 'Well, the fact is . . . I mean, I don't personally believe in these things myself but . . . well, some say the house is, well, haunted.'

They both laughed. 'Haunted! I've always wanted to live in a haunted house,' cried Elizabeth, clapping her hands together with amusement.

'You didn't notice anything, then?' Mr Wilcox asked almost timidly.

Phillip answered: 'Such as?'

'Well, I don't know. Some people who have been round it say the house has a definite atmosphere. In fact, to be quite frank with you, I showed a young couple like yourselves round it recently and afterwards they told me, and I quote, that it gave them the creeps. Couldn't see it myself but there we are. Before you decide, you ought to talk to a neighbour, a retired doctor called Hadley, he's—'

'Well, I don't think I'll bother with that, thank you,' Phillip interrupted sharply. 'Like you, I don't believe all that stuff.' He looked at his watch and said it was time they returned to London. He made an offer for Rose Cottage which was considerably less than the asking price. Even Phillip was surprised when Mr Wilcox replied instantly and without thought: 'Accepted.'

'Don't you want to consult the vendor?' asked Phillip.

'No, it's an executors' sale. They've left it to me. Glad to get it off the books, if you really want to know.'

As they drove back to London they said little, working out in their minds their respective plans for Rose Cottage. As they approached the yellow street lighting of the outer suburbs, Emma spoke for the first time on the journey.

'Some of the little children brought red roses for the school and Miss Stevenson put them in pots and they grew again in the garden. That's why she had such lovely roses.'

'Oh really,' answered Elizabeth, preoccupied with wallpapers for the upstairs bedrooms. 'Is that what Mr Wilcox told you? What a nice story.' Her thoughts returned to the problem of the main bedroom. It might have to be painted white, paper might not go with oak beams . . .

As they slowed for traffic lights Phillip wondered what sort of mortgage he would succeed in raising on such an old house.

The Sheldons were an efficient couple. As a solicitor he was able to carry out his own conveyancing on the house. In the meantime, she was responsible for organizing builders. She made several trips to the house to supervise the work which was duly completed a mere two weeks after the target date. After staying with friends for a few weeks, they moved into Rose Cottage.

This time, Emma displayed no reluctance to return to the house; if anything, she seemed to look forward to it. She also started at the village school.

About a fortnight later, on a cold morning in spring, over breakfast in the warm kitchen, Emma said: 'Don't want to go to school today.'

Phillip continued reading his newspaper, while Elizabeth sewed a name-tag into Emma's coat. Emma sat at the table pouting. Her rust-coloured hair that fell to her shoulders gleamed in the weak sunlight from the kitchen window. She repeated herself and finally elicited a response.

'Why not?' asked her mother, continuing to sew.

'Miss Stevenson told me not to,' came the brief reply.

'Who is Miss Stevenson?' asked Elizabeth, biting the thread with her teeth and wrenching away the loose end. 'There! That's another one done.' She held up the coat and admired her handiwork.

'Miss Stevenson lives *here*,' replied Emma impatiently. 'You know.'

'What on earth are you talking about, child?' said Elizabeth, taking an interest for the first time. 'A Miss Stevenson used to live here but she's, well, she went to heaven, didn't she?'

'No she didn't,' Emma shouted. Her face began to match the colour of her hair. She was normally quite pale. 'She didn't, she didn't, she's here!'

At last, Phillip lowered his newspaper. 'What's the matter with her now?'

Elizabeth put her arm around Emma's shoulders. 'Now, darling, you are going to school today, and that's that. I don't want to hear any more nonsense about Miss Stevenson. Has someone at school been telling you stories about her?'

A look of panic crossed Emma's face. She gulped, as if for air, jumped off her chair and ran towards the stairs.

'How extraordinary,' said Phillip, looking at his wife. 'Has she ever done that before?'

'No, not since her first day at that other school. What are we going to do?'

'Sent her to school, of course. There's nothing wrong with her.'

Elizabeth thought for a moment. 'The trouble is, Phillip, she does seem to have a thing about this Miss Stevenson. I've heard her holding conversations with someone in her room, and sometimes by the fireplace in the sitting-room.'

'Oh, all children do that,' said Phillip scornfully.

'Yes, that's what I thought. But something's odd. She recited her two-times table the other day in her room. She didn't know I was listening the other side of the door. And she knows her alphabet, and I know for certain that she hasn't got round to these things yet at school.'

Phillip wasn't convinced. 'It's play-acting,' he said, standing up. 'She just doesn't want to go to school. We'd better put a stop to it now.' He started to walk upstairs, beckoning Elizabeth to follow him.

The white-painted door to Emma's room was closed. Phillip was about to turn the handle when he heard a child's voice. He listened carefully.

Emma was saying: 'They told me I *had* to go to school.'

There was a long pause. Phillip and Elizabeth held their heads against the door as closely as possible without making a noise.

Emma began speaking again: 'No, I won't, I promise.'

Her parents heard a chair scraping across the floorboards, and then Emma spoke again: 'Once two is two, two twos are four, three twos are six, four twos are eight . . .'

Phillip turned the handle and pushed his way into the room. Emma was sitting on the bed surrounded by exercise books. She held a pen in her hand. No one else was in the room. Emma smiled innocently. 'Hallo, Daddy, I'm just doing my tables.'

'Yes, so I can see. Now put your coat on and Mummy will take you to school.'

'But I'm doing my lessons,' replied Emma with a frightened look on her face.

Phillip advanced towards the bed, reached down and smacked Emma on the leg. 'You'll do as you're told.'

Emma began crying. 'Miss Stevenson said I wasn't to.' She put a hand up to her face as if to staunch the flow of tears.

Phillip knelt by the bed and said firmly: 'There is no Miss Stevenson any more, do you understand, Emma?'

Emma pointed to a chair by the window. 'That's Miss Stevenson,' she said, quietly sobbing. 'She teaches me things.'

Phillip got up and walked over to the chair. He swept an arm across the seat. 'There, you see, nothing. There is no one there. It's just pretend. Now do you believe us?'

Emma's eyes widened. 'She is there, she is,' she repeated.

Phillip was becoming exasperated. He looked at his watch. 'Damn! I've missed my train.' He wagged a finger at Emma. 'You are going to school if I have to drag you there.'

Emma stared fearfully at the chair by the window. She seemed for a moment to be filled with terror. She began gasping for breath, her tiny chest heaving as she fought for air. The whites of her normally grey-blue eyes bulged slightly and the colour drained from her face. To her parents' astonishment she began to convulse.

'Christ, she's having a fit,' yelled Phillip. He urged Elizabeth to run down the lane to fetch their neighbour, Dr Hadley. Meanwhile, Phillip tried to loosen Emma's jersey. She had successively gone white, yellow and purple. Now she was grey. Suddenly, he was pushed aside by a scruffily dressed man who stood over Emma and felt her pulse. She was still shaking but not so violently. Dr Hadley pulled a blanket over Emma, turned and said: 'I'll be downstairs to see you in a moment.'

Phillip and Elizabeth took the hint and went downstairs to the sitting-room. After what seemed an inordinately long time—though it was only ten minutes—Dr Hadley joined them. He was wearing a worn tweed jacket, rough trousers and mudstained boots. He was almost bald but had a pleasant weather-beaten face and a friendly manner.

'You caught me gardening,' he said, as if reading their thoughts. 'She's all right now. She's asleep. Has she had fits for long?'

'Never,' replied Elizabeth.

'Any history of epilepsy?'

'Good heavens no!' exclaimed Phillip. 'Nothing like that.'

'We had a little chat before she went off to sleep,' said Dr Hadley.

'Did she mention how it all started?' asked Phillip.

Dr Hadley nodded. 'Very interesting, very interesting.'

'You don't believe all this nonsense, do you? Surely it's absurd to think this house is haunted by Miss Stevenson?' Phillip now seemed angry.

Dr Hadley smiled. 'Maybe, but I tend to keep an open mind.'

Phillip failed to notice this subtle rebuke and might have been rude had not Dr Hadley continued: 'You see, I knew Miss Stevenson well. She was a very strong-willed woman. If the house is haunted I can't say I'm surprised that it's her and not her sister. There are several people in the village who say they've felt her presence though no one has ever seen her—until now.'

Phillip was startled. 'So you do believe her?'

'I'm not saying that, but your daughter tells me she is here and that she gives her lessons. And there are one or two things she told me about the sisters that could only have come from them.'

'Such as, Doctor?' Elizabeth wanted to know.

'Well, Emma told me that there had once been a little girl at the school just like her, with red hair and even the same colour eyes. Indeed there was. I remember the girl quite well, I once gave her a jab for something or other. There's a quite astonishing likeness. Now, only Miss Stevenson could have told her that. She also mentioned a little boy who kept climbing the hop poles in the next field and how the farmer chased him away. Now that happened twenty years ago. Did you know any of that?'

Phillip was shocked for a moment. He glanced at Elizabeth who said: 'There was that story about the red roses, Phillip. Do you remember, in the car on our way back to London after we'd bought the house? I didn't think anything of it at the time but thinking back, how on earth could she have known about the roses?'

'The roses the children brought and which Miss Stevenson quickly repotted and later planted in the garden?' asked Dr Hadley.

'Yes,' Elizabeth answered.

'They were famous for miles around, those roses. They came from the children of a local rose grower. Miss Stevenson couldn't afford to buy his roses herself, so she used the cuttings the children brought. She was no fool.'

Phillip now felt less certain about it all. He had never believed in ghosts, and still didn't, but he was no longer quite so confident in his scepticism. 'If all this is true,' he said slowly, 'then Emma must have first met Miss Stevenson the day we saw over the house.'

'It does explain a lot of things we were too busy to notice at the time,' said Elizabeth.

After a pause, Dr Hadley asked: 'What are you going to do? These fits are no good for her at all.'

'Well, it seems to me,' replied Phillip thoughtfully, 'that we have three alternatives: we can move house; we can take her to a psychiatrist, or,' he paused for a moment, 'or, we can bring in an exorcist.'

Rather than uproot themselves again they decided to take Emma to see a psychiatrist in London. She spent three sessions with him, all of which failed to remove the notion of Miss Stevenson inhabiting Rose Cottage as a ghost. The psychiatrist said helplessly that he had never before met a child with such fixed ideas, and that perhaps Rose Cottage was haunted after all. He recommended an exorcist.

This led the Sheldons to their local vicar, a man brimming with sympathy, but offering little hope. 'I knew Miss Stevenson well,' he told them. 'A dear old soul. I can't believe she haunts the place, though I have heard tales, gossip, you know.'

When they persisted he agreed to ask a clergyman in another parish who specialized in exorcism. 'A clear case of possession by an evil spirit must be proved, though,' he warned. 'He'll also have to get the permission of the bishop.'

After the late, cold spring, summer eventually arrived. Phillip worked in the garden at weekends and evenings clearing the undergrowth, digging the vegetable patch and uncovering the famous roses. Phillip had to admit that in full bloom there were some magnificent specimens. Emma helped him sometimes as best she could. She had not been to school for two months. Illness had been the excuse. Now that it was summer she spent many days in a wild part of the garden that she called her own. She had demanded that this area should be left untouched. The wild meadow grass grew high there and Emma could play in her secret garden without being overlooked.

Although Emma had not been to school she was still receiving an education. She allowed her mother to teach her at home but only those subjects not covered by Miss Stevenson.

Reluctantly her parents went along with this, fearful of another scene like that in the spring. But they found they were no longer sleeping as soundly as they did once. Elizabeth needed sleeping tablets for the first time in her life, and Phillip's work began to suffer.

131

On warm days Emma took her lessons with Miss Stevenson hidden from view in her own patch of the garden. This she would do punctually at nine with a break for lunch at twelve-thirty, returning to lessons at two until four o'clock. Sometimes Emma would take Miss Stevenson a small gift like an apple.

One morning, as Phillip was about to leave for the station, a letter arrived from the local vicar. He regretted that the bishop had refused permission for an exorcism as it was not felt that the little girl or the house were in any way possessed. Instead, he advised medical treatment.

Phillip slumped into an armchair. 'Well, that's it then,' he said dejectedly. 'We'll have to move again.'

Elizabeth agreed, and without Emma realizing, arrangements were made to put the house on the market. Two days later, Mr Wilcox arrived unexpectedly to view the house. They were surprised to see him as the intention had been to hide the visit from Emma. Mr Wilcox strode into the sitting-room and gazed around him admiringly.

'You have done a lot to the old place,' he said with a broad smile. 'Country life too dull for you, eh?'

Before they could answer, Emma appeared at the doorway from the kitchen. Mr Wilcox grinned at her. 'Hallo, little girl, I can't remember your name but I remember you very well. With that lovely red hair of yours.'

'Emma, say hallo to Mr Wilcox,' said Elizabeth wearily, at the same time wondering how her daughter would react.

Emma said nothing but glared at Mr Wilcox who seemed taken aback by such obvious hostility. Phillip decided to tell the truth. 'Emma, you remember Mr Wilcox don't you? He sold us Rose Cottage. Well, now we've decided to move again, probably back to London. It will be fun to see your old friends again won't it?'

But there was no conviction in his face and Emma could see through it. After staring at nothing in particular in front of her for a few moments she turned on her heels and rushed from the room. They could hear her clumping upstairs.

Mr Wilcox tried to reassure. 'Moving always unsettles them at that age,' he said hastily. 'Now let's get down to—'

He was interrupted by a piercing scream from above, a cry that seemed far too loud and penetrating for a child of five.

'Emma!' shouted Elizabeth, and ran towards the stairs, followed by Phillip and Mr Wilcox. They found Emma screaming hysterically on the bed, turning and twisting her frail little body as if trying to wriggle free from some awful bondage.

'Oh God!' said Phillip, running a hand through his hair. 'Get Dr Hadley.'

Mr Wilcox disappeared, and returned a few minutes later with the retired doctor who gripped Emma's shoulders and shouted: 'It's all right, you're not leaving here. Understand? You're not going away. You can stay with Miss Stevenson.'

Emma seemed, through her hysterics, to comprehend. Slowly, her body ceased its feverish activity; apart from an occasional twitch, she seemed to calm. Her eyes opened and to her parents' relief she managed a weak smile. She began sucking her thumb and turned over on her side. Within seconds she was asleep.

All four looked at each other. Mr Wilcox stood rooted to the spot, his face dripping with perspiration. They left

Emma sleeping and crept downstairs. In the sitting-room Dr Hadley apologized. 'I'm afraid it was the only quick way I could think of getting her to stop. I must confess I was surprised that it worked so rapidly.'

'But does that mean we can't move now?' asked Phillip, with a note of desperation in his voice.

'I'd leave it for a bit if I were you,' advised Dr Hadley. 'She might grow out of it, you never know.'

A day later, after much discussion, the Sheldons abandoned the idea of leaving Rose Cottage. They resigned themselves to their predicament. They would have to compromise. After breakfast, Elizabeth stood up, looked at her watch and said: 'Come on, Emma, you're late for your lessons. Miss Stevenson will be cross.'

The Call

ROBERT WESTALL

I'm rota-secretary of our local Samaritans. My job's to see our office is staffed twenty-four hours a day, 365 days a year. It's a load of headaches, I can tell you. And the worst headache for any branch is overnight on Christmas Eve.

Christmas night's easy; plenty have had enough of family junketings by then; nice to go on duty and give your stomach a rest. And New Year's Eve's OK, because we have Methodists and other teetotal types. But Christmas Eve . . .

Except we had Harry Lancaster.

In a way, Harry *was* the branch. Founder-member in 1963. A marvellous director all through the sixties. Available on the phone, day or night. Always the same quiet, unflappable voice, asking the right questions, soothing over-excited volunteers.

But he paid the price.

When he took early retirement from his firm in '73, we were glad. We thought we'd see even more of him. But we didn't. He took a six-month break from Sams. When he came back, he didn't take up the reins again. He took a much lighter job, treasurer. He didn't look ill, but he looked *faded*. Too long as a Sam. director can do that to you. But we were awfully glad just to have him back. No one was gladder than Maureen, the new director. Everybody cried on Maureen's shoulder, and Maureen cried on Harry's when it got rough.

Harry was the kind of guy you wish could go on for ever. But every so often, over the years, we'd realized he wasn't going to. His hair went snow-white; he got thinner and thinner. Gave up the treasurer-ship. From doing a duty once a week, he dropped to once a month. But we still *had* him. His presence was everywhere in the branch. The new directors, leaders, he'd trained them all. They still asked themselves in a tight spot, 'What would Harry do?' And what he did do was as good as ever. But his birthday kept on coming round. People would say with horrified disbelief, 'Harry'll be *seventy-four* next year!'

And yet, most of the time, we still had in our minds the fifty-year-old Harry, full of life, brimming with new ideas. We couldn't do without that dark-haired ghost.

And the one thing he never gave up was overnight duty on Christmas Eve. Rain, hail or snow, he'd be there. Alone.

Now alone is wrong; the rules say the office must be double-staffed at all times. There are two emergency phones. How could even Harry cope with both at once?

But Christmas Eve is hell to cover. Everyone's got children or grandchildren, or is going away. And Harry had always done it alone. He said it was a quiet shift; hardly anybody ever rang. Harry's empty log-book was there to prove it; never more than a couple of long-term clients who only wanted to talk over old times and wish Harry Merry Christmas.

So I let it go on.

Until, two days before Christmas last year, Harry went down with flu. Bad. He tried dosing himself with all kinds of things; swore he was still coming. Was *desperate* to come. But Mrs Harry got in the doctor; and the doctor was adamant. Harry argued; tried getting out of bed and dressed to prove he was OK. Then he fell and cracked his head on the bedpost, and the doctor gave him a shot meant to put him right out. But Harry, raving by this time, kept trying to get up, saying he must go . . .

But I only heard about that later. As rota-secretary I had my own troubles, finding his replacement. The rule is that if the rota-bloke can't get a replacement, he does the duty himself. In our branch, anyway. But I was already doing the seven-to-ten shift that night, then driving north to my parents.

Eighteen fruitless phone-calls later, I got somebody. Meg and Geoff Charlesworth. Just married; no kids.

When they came in at ten to relieve me, they were happy. Maybe they'd had a couple of drinks in the course of the evening. They were laughing; but they were certainly fit to drive. It is wrong to accuse them, as some did, later, of having had too many. Meg gave me a Christmas kiss. She'd wound a bit of silver tinsel through her hair, as some girls do at Christmas. They'd brought long red candles to light, and mince-pies to heat up in our kitchen and eat at midnight. It was just happiness; and it *was* Christmas Eve.

Then my wife tooted our car-horn outside, and I passed out of the story. The rest is hearsay; from the log they kept, and the reports they wrote, that were still lying in the in-tray the following morning.

They heard the distant bells of the parish church, filtering through the falling snow, announcing midnight. Meg got the mince-pies out of the oven, and Geoff was just kissing her, mouth full of flaky pastry, when the emergency phone went.

Being young and keen, they both grabbed for it. Meg won. Geoff shook his fist at her silently, and dutifully logged the call. Midnight exactly, according to his new watch. He heard Meg say what she'd been carefully coached to say, like Samaritans the world over.

'Samaritans—can I help you?'

She said it just right. Warm, but not gushing. Interested, but not *too* interested. That first phrase is all-important. Say it wrong, the client rings off without speaking.

Meg frowned. She said the phrase again. Geoff crouched close in support, trying to catch what he could from Meg's ear-piece. He said afterwards the line was very bad. Crackly, very crackly. Nothing but crackles, coming and going.

Meg said her phrase the third time. She gestured to Geoff that she wanted a chair. He silently got one, pushed it in behind her knees. She began to wind her fingers into the coiled telephone-cord, like all Samaritans do when they're anxious.

Meg said into the phone, 'I'd like to help if I can.' It was good to vary the phrase, otherwise clients began to think you were a tape-recording. She added, 'My name's Meg. What can I call *you*?' You never ask for their *real* name, at that stage; always what you can call them. Often they start off by giving a false name . . .

A voice spoke through the crackle. A female voice.

'He's going to kill me. I know he's going to kill me. When he comes back.' Geoff, who caught it from a distance, said it wasn't the phrases that were so awful. It was the way they were said.

138

Cold; so cold. And certain. It left no doubt in your mind he *would* come back and kill her. It wasn't a wild voice you could hope to calm down. It wasn't a cunning hysterical voice, trying to upset you. It wasn't the voice of a hoaxer, that to the trained Samaritan ear always has that little wobble in it, that might break down into a giggle at any minute and yet, till it does, must be taken absolutely seriously. Geoff said it was a voice as cold, as real, as hopeless as a tombstone.

'Why do you think he's going to kill you?' Geoff said Meg's voice was shaking, but only a little. Still warm, still interested.

Silence. Crackle.

'Has he threatened you?'

When the voice came again, it wasn't an answer to her question. It was another chunk of lonely hell, being spat out automatically; as if the woman at the other end was really only talking to herself.

'He's gone to let a boat through the lock. When he comes back, he's going to kill me.'

Meg's voice tried to go up an octave; she caught it just in time.

'Has he *threatened* you? What is he going to do?'

'He's goin' to push me in the river, so it looks like an accident.'

'Can't you swim?'

'There's half an inch of ice on the water. Nobody could live a minute.'

'Can't you get away . . . before he comes back?'

'Nobody lives within miles. And I'm lame.'

'Can't I . . . you . . . ring the police?'

Geoff heard a click, as the line went dead. The dialling tone resumed. Meg put the phone down wearily, and suddenly shivered, though the office was over-warm, from the roaring gas-fire.

'Christ, I'm so *cold*!'

Geoff brought her cardigan, and put it round her. 'Shall I ring the duty-director, or will you?'

'You. If you heard it all.'

Tom Brett came down the line, brisk and cheerful. 'I've not gone to bed yet. Been filling the little blighter's Christmas stocking . . .'

Geoff gave him the details. Tom Brett was everything a good duty-director should be. Listened without interrupting; came back solid and reassuring as a house.

'Boats don't go through the locks this time of night. Haven't done for twenty years. The old alkali steamers used to, when the alkali-trade was still going strong. The locks are only manned nine till five nowadays. Pleasure-boats can wait till morning. As if anyone would be moving a pleasure-boat this weather . . .'

'Are you *sure*?' asked Geoff doubtfully.

'Quite sure. Tell you something else—the river's nowhere near freezing over. Runs past my back-fence. Been watching it all day, 'cos I bought the lad a fishing-rod for Christmas, and it's not much fun if he can't try it out. You've been *had*, old son. Some Christmas joker having you on. Goodnight!'

'Hoax call,' said Geoff heavily, putting the phone down. 'No boats going through locks. No ice on the river. Look!' He pulled back the curtain from the office window. 'It's still quite warm out—the snow's melting, not even lying.'

Meg looked at the black wet road, and shivered again. 'That was no hoax. Did you think that voice was a hoax?'

'We'll do what the boss-man says. Ours not to reason why . . . '

He was still waiting for the kettle to boil, when the emergency phone went again.

The same voice.

'But he *can't* just push you in the river and get away with it!' said Meg desperately.

'He can. I always take the dog for a walk last thing. And there's places where the bank is crumbling and the fence's rotting. And the fog's coming down. He'll break a bit of fence, then put the leash on the dog, and throw it in after me. Doesn't matter whether the dog drowns or is found wanderin'. Either'll suit *him*. Then he'll ring the police an' say I'm missin' . . . '

'But why should he *want* to? What've you *done*? To deserve it?'

'I'm gettin' old. I've got a bad leg. I'm not much use to him. He's got a new bit o' skirt down the village . . . '

'But can't we . . . '

'All you can do for me, love, is to keep me company till he comes. It's lonely . . . That's not much to ask, is it?'

'Where *are* you?'

Geoff heard the line go dead again. He thought Meg looked like a corpse herself. White as a sheet. Dull dead eyes, full of pain. Ugly, almost. How she would look as an old woman, if life was rough on her. He hovered, helpless, desperate, while the whistling kettle wailed from the warm Samaritan kitchen.

'Ring Tom again, for Christ's sake,' said Meg, savagely.

Tom's voice was a little less genial. He'd got into bed and turned the light off . . .

'Same joker, eh? Bloody persistent. But she's getting her facts wrong. No fog where I am. Any where you are?'

'No,' said Geoff, pulling back the curtain again, feeling a nitwit.

'There were no fog warnings on the late-night weather forecast. Not even for low-lying districts . . .'

'No.'

'Well, I'll try to get my head down again. But don't hesitate to ring if anything *serious* crops up. As for this other lady . . . if she comes on again, just try to humour her. Don't argue—just try to make a relationship.'

In other words, thought Geoff miserably, don't bother me with *her* again.

But he turned back to a Meg still frantic with worry. Who would not be convinced. Even after she'd rung the local British Telecom weather summary, and was told quite clearly the night would be clear all over the Eastern Region.

'I want to know where she *is*. I want to know where she's ringing from . . .'

To placate her, Geoff got out the large-scale Ordnance-Survey maps that some offices carry. It wasn't a great problem. The Ousam was a rarity; the only canalized river with locks for fifty miles around. And there were only eight sets of locks on it.

'These four,' said Geoff, 'are right in the middle of towns and villages. So it can't be *them*. And there's a whole row of Navigation cottages at Sutton's Lock, and I know they're occupied, so it can't be *there*. And this last one—Ousby Point—is right on the sea and it's all docks and stone quays—there's no river-bank to crumble. So it's either Yaxton Bridge, or Moresby Abbey locks . . .'

The emergency phone rang again. There is a myth among old Samaritans that you can tell the quality of the incoming call by the sound of the phone-bell. Sometimes it's lonely, sometimes cheerful, sometimes downright frantic. Nonsense, of course. A bell is a bell is a bell . . .

But this ringing sounded so cold, so dreary, so dead, that for a second they both hesitated and looked at each other with dread. Then Meg slowly picked the phone up; like a bather hesitating on the bank of a cold grey river.

It was the voice again.

'The boat's gone through. He's just closing the lock gates. He'll be here in a minute . . . '

'What kind of boat is it?' asked Meg, with a desperate attempt at self-defence.

The voice sounded put-out for a second, then said, 'Oh, the usual. One of the big steamers. The *Lowestoft*, I think. Aye, the lock-gates are closed. He's coming up the path. Stay with me, love. Stay with me . . . '

Geoff took one look at his wife's grey, frozen, horrified face, and snatched the phone from her hand. He might be a Samaritan; but he was a husband, too. He wasn't sitting and watching his wife being screwed by some vicious hoaxer.

'Now *look*!' he said. 'Whoever you are! We want to help. We'd like to help. But stop feeding us lies. I know the *Lowestoft*. I've been aboard her. They gave her to the Sea-scouts, for a headquarters. She hasn't got an engine any more. She's a hulk. She's never moved for years. Now let's cut the cackle . . . '

The line went dead.

'Oh, *Geoff*!' said Meg.

'Sorry. But the moment I called her bluff, she rang off. That *proves* she's a hoaxer. All those old steamers were broken up for scrap, except the *Lowestoft*. She's a *hoaxer*, I tell you!'

143

'Or an old lady who's living in the past. Some old lady who's muddled and lonely and frightened. And you shouted at her . . . '

He felt like a murderer. It showed in his face. And she made the most of it.

'Go out and find her, Geoff. Drive over and see if you can find her . . . '

'And leave you alone in the office? Tom'd have my guts for garters . . . '

'Harry Lancaster always did it alone. I'll lock the door. I'll be all right. Go on, Geoff. She's lonely. Terrified.'

He'd never been so torn in his life. Between being a husband and being a Samaritan. That's why a lot of branches won't let husband and wife do duty together. We won't, now. We had a meeting about it; afterwards.

'Go *on*, Geoff. If she does anything silly, I'll never forgive myself. She might chuck herself in the river . . . '

They both knew. In our parts, the river or the drain is often the favourite way; rather than the usual overdose. The river seems to *call* to the locals, when life gets too much for them.

'Let's ring Tom again . . . '

She gave him a look that withered him and Tom together. In the silence that followed, they realized they were cut off from their duty-director, from *all* the directors, from *all* help. The most fatal thing, for Samaritans. They were poised on the verge of the ultimate sin; going it alone.

He made a despairing noise in his throat; reached for his coat and the car-keys. 'I'll do Yaxton Bridge. But I'll not do Moresby Abbey. It's a mile along the towpath in the dark. It'd take me an hour . . . '

He didn't wait for her dissent. He heard her lock the

office door behind him. At least she'd be safe behind a locked door . . .

He never thought that telephones got past locked doors.

He made Yaxton Bridge in eight minutes flat, skidding and correcting his skids on the treacherous road. Lucky there wasn't much traffic about.

On his right, the River Ousam beckoned, flat, black, deep and still. A slight steam hung over the water, because it was just a little warmer than the air.

It was getting on for one, by the time he reached the lock. But there was still a light in one of the pair of lock-keeper's cottages. And he knew at a glance that this wasn't the place. No ice on the river; no fog. He hovered, unwilling to disturb the occupants. Maybe they were in bed, the light left on to discourage burglars.

But when he crept up the garden path, he heard the sound of the TV, a laugh, coughing. He knocked.

An elderly man's voice called through the door, 'Who's there?'

'Samaritans. I'm trying to find somebody's house. I'll push my card through your letter-box.'

He scrabbled frantically through his wallet in the dark. The door was opened. He passed through to a snug sitting-room, a roaring fire. The old man turned down the sound of the TV. The wife said he looked perished, and the Samaritans did such good work turning out at all hours, even at Christmas. Then she went to make a cup of tea.

He asked the old man about ice, and fog, and a lock-keeper who lived alone with a lame wife. The old man shook his head. 'Couple who live next door's got three young kids . . .'

145

'Wife's not lame, is she?'

'Nay—a fine-lookin' lass wi' two grand legs on her . . .'

His wife, returning with the tea-tray, gave him a *very* old-fashioned look. Then she said, 'I've sort of got a memory of a lock-keeper wi' a lame wife—this was years ago, mind. Something not nice . . . but your memory goes, when you get old.'

'We worked the lock at Ousby Point on the coast, all our married lives,' said the old man apologetically. 'They just let us retire here, 'cos the cottage was goin' empty . . .'

Geoff scalded his mouth, drinking their tea, he was so frantic to get back. He did the journey in seven minutes; he was getting used to the skidding, by that time.

He parked the car outside the Sam. office, expecting her to hear his return and look out. But she didn't.

He knocked; he shouted to her through the door. No answer. Frantically he groped for his own key in the dark, and burst in.

She was sitting at the emergency phone, her face greyer than ever. Her eyes were far away, staring at the blank wall. They didn't swivel to greet him. He bent close to the phone in her hand and heard the same voice, the same cold hopeless tone, going on and on. It was sort of . . . hypnotic. He had to tear himself away, and grab a message pad. On it he scrawled, 'WHAT'S HAPPENING? WHERE IS SHE?'

He shoved it under Meg's nose. She didn't respond in any way at all. She seemed frozen, just listening. He pushed her shoulder, half angry, half frantic. But she was wooden, like a statue. Almost as if she was in a trance.

In a wave of husbandly terror, he snatched the phone from her.

It immediately went dead.

He put it down, and shook Meg. For a moment she recognized him and smiled, sleepily. Then her face went rigid with fear.

'Her husband was in the house. He was just about to open the door where she was . . . '

'Did you find out where she was?'

'Moresby Abbey lock. She told me in the end. I got her confidence. Then *you* came and ruined it . . . '

She said it as if he was suddenly her enemy. An enemy, a fool, a bully, a murderer. Like all men. Then she said, 'I must go to her . . . '

'And leave the office unattended? That's *mad.*' He took off his coat with the car-keys, and hung it on the office door. He came back and looked at her again. She still seemed a bit odd, trance-like. But she smiled at him and said, 'Make me a quick cup of tea. I must go to the loo, before she rings again.'

Glad they were friends again, he went and put the kettle on. Stood impatiently waiting for it to boil, tapping his fingers on the sink-unit, trying to work out what they should do. He heard Meg's step in the hallway. Heard the toilet flush.

Then he heard a car start up outside.

His car.

He rushed out into the hall. The front door was swinging letting in the snow. Where his car had been, there were only tyre-marks.

He was terrified now. Not for the woman. For Meg.

He rang Tom Brett, more frightened than any client Tom Brett had ever heard.

He told Tom what he knew.

'Moresby Locks,' said Tom. 'A lame woman. A murdering husband. Oh, my God. I'll be with you in five.'

'The exchange are putting emergency calls through to Jimmy Henry,' said Tom, peering through the whirling wet flakes that were clogging his windscreen-wipers. 'Do you know what way Meg was getting to Moresby Locks?'

'The only way,' said Geoff. 'Park at Wylop Bridge and walk a mile up the towpath.'

'There's a short cut. Down through the woods by the Abbey, and over the lock-gates. Not a lot of people know about it. I think we'll take that one. I want to get there before she does . . .'

What the hell do you think's going on?'

'I've got an *idea*. But if I told you, you'd think I was out of my tiny shiny. So I won't. All I want is your Meg safe and dry, back in the Sam. office. And nothing in the log that headquarters might see . . .'

He turned off the by-pass, into a narrow track where hawthorn bushes reached out thorny arms and scraped at the paintwork of the car. After a long while, he grunted with satisfaction, clapped on the brakes and said, 'Come on.'

They ran across the narrow wooden walkway that sat precariously on top of the lock-gates. The flakes of snow whirled at them, in the light of Tom's torch. Behind the gates, the water stacked up, black, smooth, slightly steaming because it was warmer than the air. In an evil way, it called to Geoff. So easy to slip in, let the icy arms embrace you, slip away . . .

Then they were over, on the towpath. They looked left, right, listened.

Footsteps, woman's footsteps, to the right. They ran that way.

Geoff saw Meg's walking back, in its white raincoat . . .

And beyond Meg, leading Meg, another back, another woman's back. The back of a woman who limped.

A woman with a dog. A little white dog . . .

For some reason, neither of them called out to Meg. Fear of disturbing a Samaritan relationship, perhaps. Fear of breaking up something that neither of them understood. After all, they could afford to be patient now. They had found Meg safe. They were closing up quietly on her, only ten yards away. No danger . . .

Then, in the light of Tom's torch, a break in the white-painted fence on the river side.

And the figure of the limping woman turned through the gap in the fence, and walked out over the still black waters of the river.

And like a sleepwalker, Meg turned to follow . . .

They caught her on the very brink. Each of them caught her violently by one arm, like policemen arresting a criminal. Tom cursed, as one of his feet slipped down the bank and into the water. But he held on to them, as they all swayed on the brink, and he only got one very wet foot.

'What the hell am I doing here?' asked Meg, as if waking from a dream. 'She was talking to me. I'd got her confidence . . .'

'Did she tell you her name?'

'Agnes Todd.'

'Well,' said Tom, 'here's where Agnes Todd used to live.'

There were only low walls of stone, in the shape of a

house. With stretches of concrete and old broken tile in between. There had been a phone, because there was still a telegraph pole, with a broken junction-box from which two black wires flapped like flags in the wind.

'Twenty-one years ago, Reg Todd kept this lock. His lame wife Agnes lived with him. They didn't get on well—people passing the cottage heard them quarrelling. Christmas Eve, 1964, he reported her missing to the police. She'd gone out for a walk with the dog, and not come back. The police searched. There was a bad fog down that night. They found a hole in the railing, just about where we saw one; and a hole in the ice, just glazing over. They found the dog's body next day; but they didn't find her for a month, till the ice on the River Ousam finally broke up.

'The police tried to make a case of it. Reg Todd *had* been carrying on with a girl in the village. But there were no marks of violence. In the end, she could have fallen, she could've been pushed, or she could've jumped. So they let Reg Todd go; and he left the district.'

There was a long silence. Then Geoff said, 'So you think . . . ?'

'I think nowt,' said Tom Brett, suddenly very stubborn and solid and Fenman. 'I think nowt, and that's all I *know*. Now let's get your missus home.'

Nearly a year passed. In the November, after a short illness, Harry Lancaster died peacefully in his sleep. He had an enormous funeral. The church was full. Present Samaritans, past Samaritans from all over the country, more old clients than you could count, and even two of the top brass from Slough.

But it was not till everybody was leaving the house that

Tom Brett stopped Geoff and Meg by the gate. More solid and Fenman than ever.

'I had a long chat wi' Harry,' he said, 'after he knew he was goin'. He told me. About Agnes Todd. She had rung him up on Christmas Eve. Every Christmas Eve for twenty years . . . '

'Did he know she was a . . .?' Geoff still couldn't say it.

'Oh, aye. No flies on Harry. The second year—while he was still director—he persuaded the GPO to get an engineer to trace the number. How he managed to get them to do it on Christmas Eve, God only knows. But he had a way with him, Harry, in his day.'

'And . . . '

'The GPO were baffled. It was the old number of the lock-cottage all right. But the lock-cottage was demolished a year after the . . . whatever it was. Nobody would live there, afterwards. All the GPO found was a broken junction-box and wires trailin'. Just like we saw that night.'

'So he talked to her all those years . . . knowing?'

'Aye, but he wouldn't let anybody else do Christmas Eve. She was lonely, but he knew she was dangerous. Lonely an' dangerous. She wanted company.'

Meg shuddered. 'How could he bear it?'

'He was a Samaritan . . . '

'Why didn't he tell anybody?'

'Who'd have believed him?'

There were half a dozen of us in the office this Christmas Eve. Tom Brett, Maureen, Meg and Geoff, and me. All waiting for . . .

It never came. Nobody called at all.

'Do you think?' asked Maureen, with an attempt at a smile, her hand to her throat in a nervous gesture, in the weak light of dawn.

'Aye,' said Tom Brett. 'I think we've heard the last of her. Mebbe Harry took her with him. Or came back for her. Harry was like that. The best Samaritan I ever knew.'

His voice went funny on the last two words, and there was a shine on those stolid Fenman eyes. He said, 'I'll be off then.' And was gone.

Acknowledgements

Vivien Alcock: 'The Rivals', copyright © 1983 Vivien Alcock, first published in *Spooky: Stories of the Supernatural*, edited by Pamela Lonsdale (Thames/Methuen, 1983), reprinted by permission of John Johnson Ltd.

Ruskin Bond: 'The Monkeys' from *The Night Train at Delhi and Other Stories*, reprinted by permission of the author and Penguin Books India (Pty) Ltd.

Redvers Brandling: 'Mayday!', copyright © 1994 Redvers Brandling, first published in *The Young Oxford Book of Ghost Stories* (OUP, 1994), reprinted by permission of the author.

Stephen Dunstone: 'Fat Andy', copyright © 1990 Stephen Dunstone from *The Man in Black: Macabre Stories from 'Fear on Four'* (BBC Books, 1990), by permission of Lemon, Unna & Durbridge on behalf of the author.

Adèle Geras: 'Carlotta', copyright © 1994 Adèle Geras, first published in *The Young Oxford Book of Ghost Stories* (OUP, 1994), reprinted by permission of the author, c/o Laura Cecil Literary Agency.

John Gordon: 'Little Black Pies' from *Catch Your Death* (Patrick Hardy Books, 1984), by permission of A. P. Watt on behalf of the author.

Grace Hallworth: 'The Guitarist', copyright © 1984 Grace Hallworth, from *Mouth Open, Story Jump Out* (Methuen Children's Books, 1984), reprinted by permission of Marilyn Malin on behalf of the author.

Julia Hawkes-Moore: 'The Chocolate Ghost', copyright © 1994 Julia Hawkes-Moore, this version first published in *The Young Oxford Book of Ghost Stories* (OUP, 1994) reprinted by permission of the author.

Gerald Kersh: 'The Scene of the Crime' from *Sad Road to the Sea* (Heinemann, 1947).

Jan Mark: 'In Black and White', copyright © 1991 Jan Mark, from *In Black and White and Other Stories* (Viking, 1991), reprinted by permission of Penguin Books Ltd and David Higham Associates.

Alison Prince: 'The Servant' from *The Green Ghost and Other Ghost Stories*, edited by Mary Danby (Collins, 1989), reprinted by permission of Jennifer Luithlen on behalf of the author.

Lennox Robinson: 'A Pair of Muddy Shoes' from *Fear Fear Fear* (*Ernest Benn*).

Michael Vestey: 'An Apple for Miss Stephenson' from *The After Midnight Ghost Book*, edited by James Hale (Barrie & Jenkins, 1980), reprinted by permission of Random House Group Ltd.

Robert Westall: 'The Call', copyright © 1989 Robert Westall, from *The Call and Other Stories* (Viking, 1989), reprinted by permission of Penguin Books Ltd.

While every effort has been made to trace and contact copyright holders, this has not always been possible. If notified the publisher will be pleased to rectify any errors or omissions at the earliest opportunity.